THE HERDSMAN

LEE EVERETT

PROLOGUE

He sat with his head resting in his hand, despaired and despondent, wondering if it was all worth it, while afraid to admit to himself that it wasn't.

The air was ominously still as the sounds of the night dissipated and the day began to crack through the sky. It was going to be warm today, like those of the most recent past. But with the familiar weather came the familiar threat of failure, which, despite the weather, never seemed to go away.

He had already been working several hours by the time the first shards of sunlight began to peek over the horizon, which was nothing new for him. The ranch had not only become his life, but now it had become his burden. Since he now knew that nothing he did was going to make a difference in helping him save this place, his efforts didn't seem as important as they once did.

He had learned that all of his hard work, no

matter how consistent, was useless and had taken over his entire life. So why bother? In fact, things had become so busy lately that he seemed to be getting even less sleep than before. It seemed no matter how hard he worked, there was never enough time in the day to get everything done that was required of him.

His days now ran together like an endless bad dream that he was forced to relive over and over again and could never wake up from. The truth was, what was once a dream had now turned into a nightmare. And that nightmare always ended the same way, with his inevitable failure and his inability to change his fate. It was discouraging, to say the least.

He didn't understand. As time progressed and his ranch grew, he assumed the job would become easier for him, but it had turned out to be just the opposite. It seemed the more work he poured into his dream, the harder and the longer he had to work to sustain it and the less of a difference it made. How could that be?

All that effort. All that time. All of his money. And for what? To see failure inching closer and closer with each passing day, creeping up on him like a ravenous monster that he was helpless to defend himself against?

He languished in his misfortune. Money troubles were keeping him up at night. The temperature outside wasn't helping matters any, either. The weather had been warm as of late, far warmer than was expected for this time of the year since they were beginning the slow descent into fall. There was little to no breeze to speak of, making it increasingly difficult to get comfortable and to have any type of restful sleep at night.

And then there was the quiet. Restless quiet. Uncomfortable quiet. Graveyard quiet. Without wind, there were no branches moving about on the trees and nothing stirring to create any type of sound that would pierce the nighttime's deadness.

It was a quiet, haunting solitude that seemed to never end and made for a long, exhausting night without sleep, sleep that he desperately needed if he were going to have any chance of keeping a handle on the ranch and all that it demanded. He had been cursed with being a light sleeper, something that had plagued him since childhood and had only intensified as he had become an adult. The stress and worries of running a failing ranch did not make matters any better. It worked with his condition, magnifying it, causing its effects to wear on him even more than usual. As a result, the deafness of the nighttime was now his enemy, the thing he hated most and an enemy he could not afford to feed.

Even the coyote seemed to be surprisingly dormant for this time of year, their lonesome cries somehow lost in the night, not wanting to expend their limited energy to try to remain comfortable or seek out a meal, unless it was absolutely necessary.

He heard every sound, every whisper of movement, every creak of a settling foundation. It was nerve-wracking and gnawed away at his resolve. Was it because he was failing as a rancher, or because he knew he was and he wouldn't admit it to himself?

His day was the same as it had been the day before and the one before that and countless others that had become nothing but a blur to his memory, his life an endless chain of failing moments that ran together. He often wondered why he toiled away as he did, why the same routine was not producing anything new, and why his hard work and dedication and commitment had not been more adequately rewarded. But even though he wondered, he had still chosen to continue on as he had.

It wasn't fair. He had done all the right things. He had taken a chance as others had and had worked the land and put in the same amount of work as they had, possibly even more than most, but had come up short on reaping the benefits time and time again. It left him to question himself, as he had countless times before.

Was it all really worth it?

He took a break to sit outside of the barn and catch his breath. The day was just dawning and yet he was already tired, more than likely from his persistent lack of sleep. That problem had plagued him for some time now, but it had become even worse as of lately. Was it really the hard work that had caused his insomnia or was it something else?

He had been under considerable stress as of late, even more than usual. He worried about how he was going to make it. Truth be told, he hadn't been making it for some time now. Every month, it was the same old routine. He barely scraped by regardless of how much effort he put into running the place. As it stood, his ranch was barely making ends meet, much less what could be considered as thriving. He dared not back off of his work, not even a little. He wondered if it had ever been described in such a positive way.

He felt a failure for not being able to put away something for the lean months that were looming just around the corner called winter. But as it stood, these were his lean months, too. If things were this bad now, how bad would they become then?

Will pulled his handkerchief from around his neck and saturated it with the water from his canteen, wiping the back of his neck in an attempt to refresh himself as best he could as he craned his neck in an attempt to release the kinks that had formed in it. He had a lot of work ahead of him and he wondered how he was going to manage it all by himself, not that he had the extra money to hire a helper. That notion was completely out of the question.

At twenty-five years of age, Will Travis felt all the signs of a failure. He had saved his money from being on his own since the age of fifteen, with the dream of one day owning his own ranch. He had moved north from the Missouri settlement to the Montana Territory in hopes of seeking his riches. Once there, he had picked out the land he had dreamed of, placing everything he had into it and working tirelessly to make something of it. Maybe that had been his first mistake- sinking every penny he had into a dream. But there was no time to waiver. Other were right behind him, fighting for possession of the same land he wanted. If he had not been bold in his acquisition, he would have lost out. But he could see now that it had all been in vain. In the end, owning the land had made no difference. In fact, it had unknowingly sunk him into debt faster. How could he have known? The disappointment was nothing short of staggering.

How was he going to survive one more harsh winter? The truth was, he couldn't. He had reached his limit. But there had to be more. There just had to be. He couldn't see himself losing everything he had worked so hard to achieve, at least not due to failure on his part. Where was the justice in that?

He had considered taking on a partner, but the prospect was only a brief one and not one that he relished in the least. He had no desire to be indebted to any man, not by putting his ranch on the line in the process. No, if he were going to fail, then he would do it on his own terms and not by having to answer to someone else as to why.

As Will glanced out over his land, he contemplated his next move. He needed to go into town for supplies. Nothing grand, just a few necessary things to stock the kitchen. But the truth of the matter was that he dreaded these trips. They were always so stressful. So embarrassing. So degrading. But there was no way around it. He had to make the trip, regardless of how useless it made him feel. As uncomfortable as it felt, he had postponed it for as long as he could.

He had to go now, before things worsened.

CHAPTER ONE

Will Travis sighed heavily as he forced himself to stand and go inside the barn to saddle the buckskin. The horse was the only constant thing around him that he could count on- at least the only good thing. The animal had never let him down, not even once. It was also the only living thing that he had to talk to.

There had been a wife, Mable, a woman that he had met and known from back in Missouri. They had courted and after some time, he had asked her father for her hand, which he gratefully granted.

They had talked extensively about moving north to the wilderness and making a new life for themselves. They had shared stories of hope and dreams, as young couples did, that they could build and share for the rest of their lives. Eventually, they had married with the excitement of starting their new life together. Their fresh start as husband and wife had started out grand. But things had not worked out as they had hoped. It wasn't long before that excitement started to unravel.

The trip there to Montana had been long and arduous, only to find out once they had arrived that, despite all of their plans, it turned out Mabel was not cut out for frontier life, after all. Her aspirations had been big, but she did not have the fortitude to see them through. She was an anxious woman, a trait that he had not paid careful enough attention to and one that only intensified with the added stresses of beginning a new life in a strange, new place and starting from nothing. It was a situation that was doomed to failure.

Will had hoped that the excitement of being newly married would have overcome her adjustment to frontier living, but in the end, she missed the conveniences and assuredness of city life too much and all that it had to offer. Compounding things was that their first winter was exceptionally brutal, followed by a year of drought. The extremes of weather had forced her to remain cabin-bound, something she was not at tall accustomed to. It seemed as if everything compiled together to make her stay there even more difficult and incredibly unhappy the longer she stayed.

Try as he may, Will could not convince her to stick it out for better times and after a little more than a year, her love for him turned out to be not enough to cause her to stay. Instead, she packed up and returned to her family in Missouri after having wired them for the money to do so, leaving Will Travis a man heartbroken and alone, something he had yet to overcome.

After saddling the mustang, Will started for the town of Liberty. He had taken this trip numerous times, but as of late, the trip was becoming more and more strenuous. Creditors were hounding him, and for good reason. He owed them. He had not denied that in the least, for he felt it was only appropriate for a man to pay his debts, but it was difficult to pay off debts when there was nothing substantial coming in to pay with.

He avoided them whenever he hit town, but it seemed as if somehow they always knew when he arrived, or at least it felt that way. He had no money. All he could offer them was hope that things would somehow get better. But creditors did not care about hope or possibilities. That was not a form of currency. They wanted something substantial that they could use. Turns out, promises of future payments did not fit into that category.

He had thought many times of letting his ranch go back to the bank, of just letting everything go, accepting his inevitable failure and moving on, but he just couldn't pull himself to do so. Not just yet. It had taken everything he had to get it up and running and to see it all fall away to nothing was not something that he was prepared to do, at least not yet. He had already lost his wife to it. He wasn't ready to lose his dream of owning a successful ranch, too.

He had strung along his creditors to the breaking point. How much more he could convince them to carry him, he wasn't sure, but it wasn't far off.

He hit the edge of town, feeling helpless, hopeless and broke. It was only a matter of time before things came crashing down on top of him and the very same people who had gladly carried him all this time would refuse to help him any longer, not that he could blame them. They had every right to refuse his business, if it could even be called that when you didn't pay. That time was right around the corner. He could feel it. He just hoped that it wasn't going to be today.

He had friends in town, but not friends with money. They all struggled just like him, just like everyone in the territory, except it wasn't at the breaking point like him. They were not in financial straits as he was.

He had spotted some of his friends the last time he had come into town, but they had shunned him. Probably from fear that he would ask them for financial help. He had no intention of doing so, but they didn't know that and had obviously thought the worst. His dire situation had now made it awkward to see them on the streets.

As he rode deeper into town, he felt the looks of the townspeople on him as if they were judging him for his continued failures. Even though he doubted many of them knew of his financial plight, there were those who did. It would have been nice if he were wrong and it was just him being suspicious of nothing, but he knew he was not wrong. They talked about him, he already knew that, but just how much of their topics was about him and his failing ranch he wasn't sure. It was still enough to make him feel unwanted there. It didn't matter anyway, since knowing about it didn't help his situation at all. The truth was, it was better for him if he didn't know just how little they thought of him.

He stopped in front of the mercantile store and sighed, not wanting to endure what was about to happen. The owner had helped him out numerous times, and it was embarrassing and degrading for him to keep coming back to ask for even more help. He also felt bad for putting the owner in such an awkward position. He had pressed his luck here more than enough times and it was only a matter of time before his luck ran out.

He hesitated briefly, but reluctantly climbed down and tied off the buckskin before taking in a deep breath and going inside. As soon as the door opened and the clerk made eye contact with him, he felt an uneasy embarrassment take him over. The man behind the counter knew what was coming. It was the same thing that happened every time Will entered his store. He slowly walked up to the counter where the clerk was standing, waiting reluctantly.

"Morning, Jack," Will spoke first with a timid, uncomfortable smile.

"Will," the man responded dryly, as if anticipating what was about to be asked of him.

Will Travis glanced around the store to make sure none of the other couple of customers could hear their conversation before leaning in slightly in the storekeeper's direction. "Jack, I was hoping to get a couple of things."

The clerk, Jack, sighed out loud from his own awkwardness, his face falling into a familiar frown from being put in such an uncomfortable position. "Will, I'd love to help you out, but I can't let you keep doing this," he started as he also leaned in closer to Will to avoid him the embarrassment of being heard. "Besides, Will, you're behind on your account, as it is."

"I know, and I appreciate you working with me, but I just need a little more time, that's all, Jack, just a little more time."

"I don't mind helping you out, Will, but you really need to make some payments on the balance before it gets any more out of hand."

"But I just made a payment not long ago. Remember?"

Jack nodded in agreement, but his demeanor was not supporting the claim. "Yes, you did, but you only paid a small amount and it didn't even cover what you bought that same day. Plus, that was almost three weeks ago and you've made even more charges since then."

Will ran the details through his mind. He didn't remember it being that long ago, but then again, time wasn't on his side in the matter and he was sure Jack was correct with the facts since he had always been before and kept careful notes. Maybe it was just that he didn't want to admit the truth. "I didn't think it had been that long," he admitted, embarrassed and ashamed.

"I'm sorry, Will. I'd love to help you out, but I just can't keep doing this. I've got a business to run. If I did it for you, I'd have to do it for others, and pretty soon I'd be out of business myself."

Will looked around and then leaned a little closer, his voice solemn and meek. "Jack, I know I owe the money. I don't dispute that. I just need a little more time. Please, can you help me out? I know I don't deserve it, but I really think I can turn things around here really soon. What'll you say? Can you help me out, Jack?"

Jack stared at Will, mulling over the situation in his mind. "I like you, Will, but I'm sorry. Business is business." He hesitated and then sighed again as his resistance deteriorated at seeing the man's desperation. He had helped Will out before, even in dark times like these, and somehow, Will had managed to find away to come through. He had to think that he could do it again. At least that's what he was counting on. "Alright," he said with a compassionate reluctance. "I'll extend you some credit, but it's just the one time, Will, and that's it. I'm serious. If you don't work at catching your bill up, then I'm afraid I won't be able to help you anymore."

"Thank you, Jack," Will said as a wave of relief washed over him. He shook the man's hand, creating a faint smile of reward on the man's face. "I really appreciate this. I promise I'll make it up to you, with interest and I'll just get what I really need."

Jack nodded reluctantly. "Go get what you need and I'll invoice it."

Will walked into the store picking up coffee, jerky and some other things that he deemed essential and made a pile on the counter as Jack began writing them down. Will thought his list over carefully and took the opportunity to get what he thought he would also need in the near future, knowing he would not get another chance to get supplies.

Jack finished adding the items up and turned the paper around for Will to sign. Will signed, handed the paper back to Jack, and they shook hands. "I really do appreciate this, Jack."

"You're welcome." Jack gave him a faint, under-standing, sympathetic smile. "Good luck to you, Will. I mean that." Will smiled. He could tell from the man's expression that he was genuinely sincere.

He picked up the bag containing his items and nodded to Jack one final time. As he started for the door, he had mixed emotions. He had no intention of stiffing his friend for the money. He just needed a little time to get back on his feet, and some luck coming his way certainly wouldn't hurt. He was grateful that his friend had helped him out again, but he was also worried that the way things were going, he wouldn't be able to live up to his promise if that luck didn't somehow find its way to him.

CHAPTER TWO

That night, Will's conscience was even heavier and more disruptive than usual. He had gotten supplies, but he couldn't help but feel as if he had taken advantage of his friend, Jack. He wanted to pay the man and had every intuition to, but he couldn't help but feel he had stolen from the man. He went to bed feeling nothing but guilt.

Will awoke the following morning, feeling no more for the better. He had not slept the night before, which was nothing new despite his small victory at the mercantile store. Acquiring essentials should have eased his conscience, if only for a short time, but that hadn't been the case. It had only managed to make him feel worthless.

The persistent worries of owning a failing ranch, along with his building guilt over having to beg the owner of the mercantile store for essentials, were bringing him down. The stress was compelling and was getting to him, even more than usual, but try as he may, he did not have a solution to the problem.

He swung his legs over the side of the bed and planted them firmly on the old, unrelenting, cold floor. After a trip to relieve himself, he decided to cook breakfast and enjoy the few groceries he had at his disposal while he could.

After breakfast, he went out to the barn to give fresh hay to the buckskin. He had sold some of the remaining head of cattle the month before, at his reluctance, and only because he had no other choice. It was the last thing he had to bargain with, a feeling that was a disturbing notion. The feeling was surreal. Such a safety net would only last so long, and then he would be out of the goods he owned. Then what? When he needed money the next time, he had no idea where he was going to find it.

He had managed to squirrel away a small amount of cash, nothing substantial, but just enough to ensure that he would not go hungry at the last minute. Over the last few months, he had been tempted to dip into it out of desperation, but no matter how bleak things had seemed, he had declared it off limits until he was left with no other choice. It was painful to push its existence out of his mind, but it was a necessary pain that he had to endure. He could not give in to temptation. Not now. Not when he had come so far. He feared there would come a time when having the little bit of cash on hand could very well be the difference in whether or not he ate or starved.

His mind was racing, focused on trying to think of a way to turn things around, but it was the same dead-end thinking that had followed him through the time he had owned the ranch and had now led him to his current situation. For a brief instant, he considered going back to work as a cattle hand, but while it would bring money in immediately, it would do nothing to get him out of the debt he had accumulated and paying back his creditors on a ranch hand's salary wasn't going to be a quick resolution to the problem, at least not one that they were going to be accepting of.

How had this happened? He had never been lazy and had always put in an ample share of work. He had seen others with less drive and determination make something of their places and in less time. Why could he not do the same? They were no better than him and he deserved the same level of success that they had. So why had it not worked out for him as well?

Will conceded to the circumstances and decided to try to take his mind off of things, at least for a little while. He was working on repairing the corral fence when he heard several horses approaching. Visitors were few and far between out here, so any recent guests that made it out to his ranch were usually not of a social visit, but rather one of business, and usually not in a good way.

He dropped his tools and walked around the side

of the barn where he could greet whoever it was, wiping his forehead on his sleeve just as two horses came up into view in front of the house. Will's heart sank when he recognized one of the men as the president of the bank, Harland Fowler. He did not know the other man.

"Morning, Will," Fowler greeted him as the two horses came to a stop in front of him. "Good to see you again. This here is Mr. Emery Chastain," he nodded in the other man's direction. "He's in charge of the land office."

Will nodded to Fowler and then looked over at the other man. "Harland, Mr. Chastain. What brings you fellas out here?"

Harland Fowler took in a deep breath before he began. "Will, I'm afraid this isn't a trip of pleasantries. I hate to have to be the one to tell you this, but I have some bad news for you. I'm afraid the bank has called in your loan."

Will stood stunned, initially unable to process what he had just been told. He had feared this day for some time now, but had always tried to fool himself and pushed it off into the recesses of his mind that it was still a way off. "What are you talking about, Harland? I'm not that far behind. How far behind can I be? Two months?"

"Actually, Will, it's *four* months," Fowler corrected him reluctantly.

Will had a confused expression. "I guess I don't

understand, Harlan. I've been four months behind before and it was never an issue."

"Well, that's not exactly true, Will," Fowler politely corrected him as he adjusted himself in his saddle from the uneasiness of the conversation. "It *was* an issue before. We just didn't push it."

"Where is this coming from, Harland? Why all of a sudden is this now coming up?"

Fowler was uncomfortable as he quickly glanced at Chastain before he continued. "In the bank's eyes, you've become a liability. The truth is..."

"The truth is, Mr. Travis, that your ranch is failing," Emery Chastain said sternly as he took over the conversation. "That is the reality of it and the bank and the land office feel it's time to step in and act before things get anymore out of hand. In fact, we've been most lenient until now. We have every right to do so, I assure you."

Will gave the man a subdued glare. "I don't dispute that I owe the money, Mr. Chastain. I never have, but, like I said, I've been behind before."

"There in lies the problem, Mr. Travis," Emery Chastain replied. "There seems to be a history of late payments dating back for some time. As I said, the board of directors has been lenient and has chosen to overlook them until now to try to give you ample time to resolve the issues, but, so far, that hasn't worked. It appears that offering you more time has not worked. Now, I'm afraid they aren't willing to extend you any more time to try to work something out. As you are aware, we are not a charity, Mr. Travis," Chastain pointed out dryly, "or else we could not remain in business for our customers who *are* able to repay their debts."

Will felt his anger building inside him from the hidden insult and the condescending attitude, but for his own sake, he stifled it as best he could. Losing it now certainly would not help his position. "I'm not asking for charity, Mr Chastain. I'm only asking for a little more time to resolve the issue."

Chastain gave him a condescending look as he stiffened in his saddle. "I'm afraid the time for that has come and gone, Mr. Travis."

"You can't take my land away from me, Harland," Will reasoned as he turned his attention back to his friend. "It's all I've got. You know that. I've put everything I have into it. My blood and sweat built this place. If I lose it, I lose everything. I have nothing to fall back on. *Nothing.*"

"I'm sorry, Will," Harland Fowler stated sincerely, "I really am, but the board of directors has made their decision very clear and I don't have the authority to go up against them. I'm afraid it's out of my hands at this point."

"Your land will be auctioned off and any proceeds will go towards the balances of your creditors," Emery Chastain added dryly. Will could tell the man enjoyed this part of his job a little too much. "If there's any left over, it will naturally be turned back over to you."

Will ignored the man's lack of empathy as he shook his head in disbelief. "I can't believe this. I can't believe it's come down to losing everything I've built."

"Maybe you can move and start over somewhere else," Chastain flippantly suggested out of nowhere.

Will shot the man a disgruntled look. "With what, Mr. Chastain? Do you understand that there is nothing else? Everything I have is already tied up in this place. I'd literally be starting over with nothing."

"At least you're still young enough to do so," Chastain pointed out without emotion, causing Will to shoot the man a dejected glare. Harlan Fowler also gave the man a silent glance, as if wanting the man to be more compassionate.

"I'm sorry, Will," Fowler tried to assure him. "I want you to know that it's nothing personal. You know I'd help you more, if I could. I'm just doing my job, the part of my job that I hate." Will knew that was his way of saying he objected to being forced to run him off of his own land.

"I know, I don't blame you," Will responded honestly. "It's all my fault. I'm the one that got myself into this mess." He paused before asking the next and most important question. "How much time do I have?"

Fowler mulled the question over briefly before answering. "I think I can convince the board to stall eviction proceedings until after the first of the month." The comment drew a disagreeing glance from Chastain, who said nothing.

Will scoffed out loud. "That only gives me a little less than three weeks to come up with something. That's not going to do me much good."

Fowler shook his head in dismay. "I wish there was something more I could do, but I'm afraid that's the best I can offer you, Will."

"Don't you have some cattle left that you can sell, Mr. Travis?" Emery Chastain asked, his expression unsympathetic.

"Yeah, but I'm counting on them to build a herd. If I sell them, it's only a temporary fix. It doesn't do anything to solving the long-term problem. If I don't have a herd, I don't have a ranch." Will was agitated that Chastain would recommend such a ludicrous suggestion to an obvious problem. It showed that the man knew nothing of ranching, only of numbers.

"I'm sorry, Will," Fowler responded. "I wish I could do something more to help you, but, like I said, my hands are tied."

"I understand," Will replied without really meaning it. "I don't blame you." Although Harland Fowler was his friend, and he knew he was doing all he could, the man's apologies did little to help the situation.

Fowler pulled back on his reins to ready his horse. "I'll see you later, Will. And again, I'm sorry." Emery Chastain nodded without speaking as Will watched the two men ride away, his mind still trying to comprehend what had just happened. It had turned out to be the worst day ever. He had been cut off from buying supplies in town and now he had lost his ranch all on the same day.

What else could possibly go wrong?

A defeated Will Travis abandoned his work on the corral and walked over to sit down on the front porch in his rocker. There was work to be done all around him, but what was the use of doing it now? Why fix a corral that he would soon no longer be allowed to use? It would all be done for the benefit of someone else, so why bother, since a stranger or whoever else would end up with his ranch.

His ranch.

He felt sick to his stomach, thinking about losing what he had created from nothing. The house and barn that he had built with his own two hands. The corral he had constructed. The fences he had put up and mended. The hay he had harvested. The crops he had planted. The herd he had grown. All gone. Everything. The more he thought about it, the more it tore away at his gut. He was sitting by and watching everything slowly and systematically being taken away from him, and it appeared as if there was nothing he could do about it.

He removed his hat and wiped the building sweat from around his face as he sat on the front porch. This was it. There was no more stalling. This was a runaway train, and he was all out of ideas about what to do to stop it. Everything that came to mind as being a resolution was either immoral or illegal, neither of which he was interested in involving himself in. He had never stepped outside of the law before and he wasn't about to start doing so now, regardless of how desperate he was to make it all go away. Besides, he had proven not to be good at coming up with an honest solution, so there was nothing to suggest that a dishonest one would work out any better for him.

His mind suddenly went from reasoning to survival mode. He hated the concept, but it was one that he had been thrust into. He wasn't going down without putting up a fight.

He jumped up from his rocker and headed for the barn. Surely there was something of value left that he could sell to stall the sale of his ranch, something that he had somehow overlooked. It might not be anything of great value, just as long as it was something that could keep those at bay that were after his ranch.

He walked into the barn and paused. The mule was gone, had been for some time now. He had sold it the previous year when he foolishly thought things were going to get better and he could afford to buy him back, but that time had never come. His extra saddle was also gone, as were his bridles and the other tack. It didn't matter anyway since he had only the one horse. Glancing around the interior of the barn did not produce anything that he could see helping his situation, giving him the realization that his collection of belongings was as pitiful and scant as his collection of good memories.

He stepped outside and looked out over his land. It was good land, land that he had put all of his hopes and dreams into and was now being striped away as if his work had meant nothing, as if he had never been there to begin with. It was being taken away from him and not by bandits with hoods and revolvers, but by an uncaring and unsympathetic man in a suit stuffed behind a desk with nothing more than the stroke of a pen.

What a sad revelation.

The more he thought about it, the more the finality of the situation sunk in. He needed to get out of there for a while. He needed to go somewhere and collect his thoughts.

He needed a drink.

CHAPTER THREE

Will rode the buckskin into town and headed straight for the Broken Back Saloon. His entire mindset had changed in less than half of a day. He was less interested in what the townspeople thought of him now that he was probably going to lose his ranch. Its inevitable demise had soured him.

He was sure word had already started spreading of his impending doom. That was the way of a small town. Bad news always traveled faster than good news. He had held out hope that somehow he would be able to find a way to dig himself out of the hole he had made, but the visit from Harlan Fowler and Emery Chastain had changed his mind about that and sealed his fate What people thought of him was no longer a concern. In fact, a great many things were suddenly unimportant to him. *Let even one of them imply how worthless he was and see what happened.*

After tying off the buckskin, he strolled inside to

try to drink away his worries. At this point, he felt it couldn't do any more harm than what had already befallen him. At least drinking would dull his faculties and give him a few hours of peace and satisfaction, if nothing else. He looked forward to the break from the tension.

"Whiskey," he spoke as he came up to the bar. The bartender pulled a bottle from under the counter and poured a glass full and went to place it back when Will stopped him. "Leave the bottle." The bartender replaced the bottle next to him and walked away to attend to someone else while Will took the bottle and walked over to a nearby table to sit. After loosely falling into his chair, he downed the shot and immediately poured another as he stared at the batwing doors swinging ever so gently back and forth from the light breeze that floated down main street.

The air inside the saloon was thick with tobacco smoke, filth and dust. Will could see the tiny bits of dust casually floating in the few strands of sunlight that managed to creep their way just inside the door and onto the floor. It was not a clean establishment, not by any means, but it provided a refuge for those seeking to temporarily drink away their troubles. The level of sanitation the place provided would not come into play for these people. It was where he belonged.

A few customers came and went as he lost count of his drinks, while the reality of what he faced began to settle in even more. He had to come up with an alternate plan in the event that he could not come up with a plan to save his place, which was looking less likely with each passing hour. No amount of whiskey was going to make all of that go away, but he was still willing to test that theory. He was thinking about what he was going to do next, but he had no answers. He had no family, no friends that he could borrow from, and nowhere else to go. He had no prospects, no job, and no money. What was he to do?

The drained atmosphere in the saloon was the perfect place for him to sit back and stew in his own failure. The only ones typically inhabiting such a place this early in the day were the drifters who were passing through and those townspeople who had very little going for them and had nothing better to do than try to drink away their misery. He had never passed as a drunkard, but given his situation, he was willing to give it a try if it took away the hanging despair, even for a little while.

He had polished off multiple drinks when two men walked into the saloon, talking quietly amongst themselves, and took their spots at the bar a short distance away from him. Will noticed their arrival, but beyond that, he paid no attention to them. From their movements it appeared as if they had already had a head start on drinking before stepping foot in the Broken Back, one reasonably more sauced than the other.

He downed another drink and sat down the glass, blindly staring off into nowhere, savoring its texture when he overheard what the bartender said to one of the men.

"You look like you could use a drink, Ted," the bartender stated as he slid two glasses over to the men and began pouring.

"That's why we're here," the man who was with Ted answered with a hearty grin.

Apparently, the bartender sensed an uneasiness with the men, a skill he had no doubt perfected over the years. He finally decided to pry the subject from them. "Something troubling you boys?"

"Aw, it's the market," the man called Ted answered before he tossed back his drink. "Cattle prices have gone down next to nothing from what they used to be not that long ago, and it doesn't look like it's going to get better anytime soon. If they don't pick back up soon, I don't know what I'm going to do. I'm going to be in some real trouble. I sank everything I've got into them. It just isn't worth it to raise a herd, at least not like it used to be."

I know how you feel, Will thought to himself.

"You know the market always changes," the bartender stated as he tried to help. "It'll come back. You just wait and see."

"I don't know," Ted reasoned, shaking his head in disagreement. "I've ridden it through some pretty tough times over the years, but I've never seen it get this bad. I don't know if I've got it in me to ride out this stretch."

"Forget cattle," the second, more inebriated man

spoke up. "These days the real money is in horses," the second man noted as he held his glass up in salute. "Now, *there's* where your fortune lies. If you can get your hands on those, you'll make a bundle of money."

"Yeah, but where are you gonna find horses?" Ted turned to his friend and argued. "It's not that easy, y'know, Cal. They're a lot harder to come by than cattle. If they were, everybody would get some."

"Yeah, I know," the second man, Cal, snickered through a belch. "That's why you need to get 'em from that canyon everybody talks about."

The bartender's attention was peaked as he cut the man a curious glance. "What canyon you talking about, Cal?"

"It's nonsense," Ted stated definitively, cutting in. "Don't pay any attention to him. He doesn't know what he's talking about."

"Yes, I do," Cal reasoned as he tried to stand straighter now that he had all the attention, but his body would not allow him to maintain the stance, so he ended up slumped back onto the bar. "You know. The one the indians supposedly have."

"I ain't never heard of such a place, Cal," the bartender said with a questionable glare. "You sure you ain't too sauced to know what you're talking about?"

"I'm not drunk," Cal protested unconvincingly. "I know what I know and I'm telling you I hear that canyon is for real."

"Yeah, yeah, yeah, I've heard of that place," Ted registered with a nod as he finally picked up on the conversation. "But it's more legend than it is a fact. It's never been proven."

"I wonder if that legend about that canyon of wild horses really *is* for real?" The second man, Cal, asked. "Wouldn't that be nice if it was?"

"You're drunk," Ted pointed out as he drank another shot. "You're talking foolishness."

Cal nodded in agreement. "I know, but I still understand what I'm talking about."

Will had listened to the exchange with growing interest. The comments caught Will's attention, causing him to pause, taking a drink as his hand stopped in midair before it had reached his mouth. He turned to the men and listened more intently.

"Aw, don't kid yourself, Cal. That legend isn't real," the first man, Ted, replied with a dismissive wave of his hand. "If it was, you know someone would've found 'em by now. No one's going to leave a canyon full of wild horses alone, you idiot. There's too much money to be made from gathering and selling 'em. Besides, even if it was true, you and I both know that the Lakota didn't put 'em there. They would have likely got hung up in there by a storm or from an avalanche or something that blocked 'em from getting out."

"So you *do* believe it's true," Cal insisted, as he tried to catch Ted in a confession.

"No, I didn't say that," Tell explained. "All I'm

saying is there would have to be a good reason why those horses didn't get out, if there are horse, which there ain't."

"Those horses would be wild, that's for sure," Cal noted.

The bartender nodded his agreement. "Yeah, and those would be solid stock, too, since they wouldn't be allowed to breed outside of the canyon. That would make them even more valuable."

The second man, Cal, nodded in agreement, as well. "Yeah, that's what I'm saying, but even if they are real, they're still good and safe. No one wants to have to go up against the Lakota to try to get 'em, especially out of a canyon that's tight enough that its held them in all these years."

Finally, Will's curiosity got the better of him. "What canyon are you fellas talking about?" He said to the men, causing both of them to turn in his direction.

"Aw, it's nothing, mister," Ted answered dismissively with a wave. "It's just an old Indian legend, that's all. It's just wishful thinking, really. There's nothing to it. It's a lot of foolishness, that's all."

"I've never heard about it before," Will admitted as he held his bottle up for them to see. The two men gladly took the assumed offer and walked over to his table and took their seats. He poured them each a glass as he continued.

"You said it was an old Indian legend?" Will asked as he placed the bottle on the table. "I've never heard of it before. What exactly does the legend say about this valley?"

"It's an old legend about the Lakota and a canyon that they have full of wild horses," Ted started. "They watch over it and no one is allowed near it for fear that they'll be killed. It's just a stupid story, mister. I wouldn't get too excited about it if I were you. There's no proof that it even exists."

"Well, you fellas seem to hold some stock in what it means so there has to be something to it."

"Naw. That was just the liquor talking, mister. We don't really know anything about it 'cept for what we heard from others."

"What did you hear from others?"

Ted glared at Cal, but decided to field the question since Cal didn't look like he was in much shape to do so himself. "It's all a legend, mister, so I don't know how much, if any of it, is believable. I don't want you to get your hopes up and find out it's really nothing to it and be sore at us for telling you."

"Don't worry," Will said dismissively, with a soft scoff. "We're just friends talking, that's all. I'll believe what I want to believe, regardless of what you fellas tell me."

The admission helped Ted to perk up. "Well, what do you want to know?"

"Where did the horses come from? Does anyone know?" Will asked as he downed his own drink.

"Nobody knows," the second man, Cal, responded. "The legend says they have always been there as far back as anyone can remember, but I think they would have had to have been trapped in there somehow. You think about it: as much value as the indians have for horses, why would they pile a bunch of 'em up and not put 'em to use? It doesn't even make sense. Horses are necessary in this territory, especially to the indians. That's why I say it isn't true."

"Like you said, why corral them in a canyon?" Will questioned, trying to agree with Ted to help loosen his tongue. "Why not just use them?"

Ted fielded the question. "Supposedly, they are being used. There's something in the legend about the horses only being for certain warriors or they can only use them for certain riding or something like that. I can't remember exactly how it goes. The natives discovered the horses there and believe that the horses were placed there by their ancestors. Like I said, I don't know all the details. I've just heard the story told over the years, but I never gave it much credence. I think it's nothing but a bunch of nonsense, myself."

Will leaned over the edge of the table as his curiosity continued to build. "So where exactly is this canyon supposed to be located?"

Cal scoffed out loud at Will's gullible reaction. "You're not really going to believe the story, are you, mister? I'm telling 'ya it's nothing but a bunch of hogwash."

"You've got to admit, it sounds interesting, especially to someone like me," Will declared as he poured each man another round. "I wonder why I've never heard about it before."

"Because it's a fantasy, that's why."

"Still, it's something to think about."

"Well, I wouldn't put a lot of stock in it," Ted added. "Men have been looking for that canyon for years and they never found it. Never even got close. Some of 'em went as far as wandering on Lakota land to get a closer look. That was a big mistake."

"Why?" Will asked curiously. "What happened to 'em?"

Ted eyed him with a serious look. "That's just it. Nobody knows. They never came back, so tell what was real and what wasn't. But you can imagine."

Will leaned up closer. "You mean no one has ever actually seen the canyon?"

"Nope. Not and live to tell about it."

"Then how did the legend get started?"

"Nobody knows that, either."

"But if it did exist, it should be easy to find, shouldn't it? I mean, just think about how much room you would need to hide an entire canyon full of wild horses. It'd have to be of considerable size and you're telling me no one has ever claimed to have seen it?"

"Nope. Word would have spread, if they had."

Will shook his head. "I find that hard to believe. Sounds like people might have found it, but they've just been afraid to do anything about it because they're scared of the Lakota."

"They should be," Cal said while he chucked, as he downed his most recent drink. "The Lakota aren't exactly forgiving when it comes to people trespassing on their land."

"That's why they would be so protective of a valley of horses. It's because of where it is. It's on their land. The land that they hold sacred," Ted added. "If somebody did find that valley, you can bet they'd be hollerin' it from the rooftops."

"And you don't have any better directions than the fact that it's in Lakota Territory?"

"It's supposed to be on Lakota land, that's all I know," Ted answered. "Somewhere around Hangman's Gulch, from what I've heard, but probably more on the far side of it. That's another reason to leave it alone, because you'd have to cross Lakota land and Hangman's Gulch just to get to it to check it out, but I don't know how reliable that last part is. Either one of those places is enough to convince me that I don't want any part of it."

Will sat quietly, pondering the notion, but his continued lost look and his interest in the legend began to concern the two men. "Mister, you aren't really considering trying to find that canyon, are you?" The second man, Cal, spoke in a surprisingly coherent tone. "It's just a stupid legend. I don't even know if the Lakota believe it. I'd hate for something to happen to you because of a story we told you about. It ain't real."

"I don't buy that," Will insisted. "Why would they make the whole thing up so people would intentionally bother them? They would have to know that people would come looking for it. Why bring that kind of unwanted, unnecessary attention to themselves?"

"That's why I said it's just a legend," Ted noted. "Bringing that kind of attention to themselves doesn't make sense. It's a load of hooey. Nothing more."

"But it is interesting to think about, don't you agree?" Will stated. "I mean, it's not every day you hear about a canyon of wild horses just sitting there for the taking."

"They're not for the taking, mister," Ted noted solidly. "You best get that through your head. You gotta understand, you're talking about going up against the Lakota. The *Lakota*. You go in there looking for them horses and you're going to get yourself strung up and killed. And that would be a slow death, too."

Cal nodded in agreement. "Yeah, don't go getting yourself killed chasing some stupid, old legend, mister."

"Nah," Will said, trying to dismiss the theory. "I guess it was just wishful thinking, like you said. If it hasn't been found by now, it's just a legend."

"Well, you'd be better off just forgetting you ever

heard anything about it," Ted responded. "Like I said, people have tried to look for it and they come up missing. I don't suppose the Lakota are too keen on strangers trespassing on their land."

"No," Will responded with a quick smile while he poured the two men another drink as his mind began to wander. "I suppose not."

CHAPTER FOUR

Will continued talking with the two men for over another hour, serving them more shots of liquor to help loosen their tongues and trying to draw more information out of them about the legend, but they had nothing of further use to add to their story. Their suspicion about his interest in the story was eventually dulled enough from the liquor that they no longer tried to talk him out of pursuing it, which is what he wanted.

After they had successfully emptied the bottle, the two men saw no need for his company, thanked him for their drinks and staggered out the saloon door, leaving Will alone at the table to think.

He needed the time for all that he had heard to sink in. He was in no hurry to leave. Why rush back to the ranch? His mind was too preoccupied with the thought of the canyon.

He kept running the story over and over in his mind. He was no idiot to believe in such nonsense. It was probably a far-fetched notion, anyway. The story was probably nothing more than the ramblings of a drunkard who was looking to gain some friends or to impress those who they conversed with. Still, it was an elaborate attempt to gain fiends, if that were the case. And each man was equally knowledgeable about it. He would be an idiot to throw all of his energy into tracking down such a canyon.

Or would he?

He had to consider the likelihood that it existed. But the more he thought about it, the more he tried to argue himself out of the notion. But there was still a part of him that had to admit that he shouldn't dismiss it entirely. Not just yet.

The root of the legend sounded to him like it could be a plausible story. It reminded him of the gold rush from a few years earlier. No one had brought the gold back east for others to see before masses of people had left everything behind and ventured out west to see it for themselves on nothing more than rumors. That was the power of persuasion. The validity of a gold rush didn't have to be proven for people to believe. Word alone had been enough to convince them. Such was the case with this.

The legend may have sounded far-fetched, but the reality was there had to be something to it if numerous people had tried to prove it to be true and

had never been heard from again. Those circumstances weren't a coincidence. One person could
disappear without rising an eyebrow of question, but
more than one after the same canyon? It was highly
unlikely.

Those people hadn't simply vanished into thin air.
Something had taken them and prevented them from
returning. Something or, more than likely, someone.
Of course, some of that could be because they had
encountered the Lakota, who were not particularly
fond of the white man since they had broken their
treaty with the Lakota and driven them from most of
their land. Because of that, he couldn't blame them
for being untrusting.

But then again, he reasoned that someone would
have had to have seen the canyon for the rumor to
get started in the first place and for the legend to
take hold. It had to be someone other than the
Lakota. The Lakota certainly wouldn't spread rumors
about something they would want to keep quiet. And
what would an individual have to gain by coming up
with such an elaborate hoax? What would be the
purpose behind creating such a deception? To lure
people to a dangerous location in the heart of Indian
territory? To knowingly drive people to their deaths?
Why would someone go to all the trouble to do that
if there wasn't some level of truth in the claim?

The Lakota certainly wouldn't tout a canyon full
of wild horses up for the taking, knowing that there
would be those who wished to take them. Why bring

that kind of worry and trouble to themselves, knowing the white man and other tribes would descend on them like locusts?

The mystery of it all was that he had never heard of the story before and he had lived in this part of the territory his whole life. He had to wonder the validity of the claim or else why had the subject never come up before? Why hadn't anyone talked about it before now? Was it because it *was* nothing more than a silly folktale? Maybe.

Was the story real enough to be believed? The men at the bar, Ted and Cal, were under no obligation to spread such rumors if they weren't true. They had nothing to gain from it and it did not benefit them in any way to come up with such a tale, so there had to be a reason to intentionally bring up such a subject.

Will thought of the men again. They had appeared to be decent, level-headed men. They had been reasonably sober when they had entered the saloon, so their talk wasn't the babbling of a drunken stupor, either. Even Cal, as drunk as he was when he left, still maintained that what he was talking about was for real. As far as he could tell, these men were credible. But how did you go about verifying if something like that was legitimate?

Will lingered at the saloon for a while longer, not wanting to go back to his ranch. There was nothing for him there, a strange admission to make, considering it was all he had in the world. But it was the truth. All that remained of his efforts was an empty house and land with a debt he could not dare challenge.

After leaving the saloon, Will decided to make a quick stop at the livery stables. The conversation in the saloon had gotten him to thinking, and he needed some information. He had never worked with wild horses before. He had no idea how much they were worth, although he reasoned they would have to be of considerable value. A herd of horses was valuable, regardless, but how much more would a herd of wild horses be? He had to find out and, based on what he was asking, this was as good of a place to get it as anywhere. When he walked inside, he came upon a man mucking out the stalls who he took to be the owner.

"Can I help you with something, young fella?" The man asked, while taking a well-deserved moment to look up from his unpleasant task.

"I was just wondering about something and I needed to get your expert opinion."

"Well, I don't really know what I could be an expert on, but if you're willing to ask, I'm willing to listen and do my best."

"I'm looking to buy a horse," Will started. "Do you know anything about them?"

"I'v been around 'em since I was knee high, so, yeah, I'd say my knowledge on 'em is fair to middling."

"The horse I'm looking at is pure bred and wild

and comes from solid stock. Never been broken. Its parents were also wild. Can you tell me about how much something like that would be worth, so I don't get taken?"

"Completely wild, huh?" The man asked, his face somewhat distorted from concentration. "Well, if it's in good shape, it could go two-fifty to maybe even three hundred dollars. But it'd have to be good stock. I'm talking plenty of muscle and good size."

"Hmmm... Alright, well, that answers my question. Thanks for your time." Will nodded as he turned and walked back out to the buckskin. As he rode towards home, he kept running the story of the wild horses through his mind again and again. Why was he even considering pursuing this? With his current situation, why dwell on such an absurd idea? Or was it such an absurd story, after all?

And then there was the risk involved. An unnecessary risk, he might add. Many had tried to find them and they had all failed. *All* of them. What made him think that he would be any different? Others would have likely taken friends with them to help drive the herd. But he had no one. If they couldn't make it out of there as a group, how would he make it alone?

The Lakota were known for being a peaceful tribe unless provoked, and he imagined trespassing onto their land without warning and stealing their sacred horses would certainly constitute provocation. If that were the only way to get them out of the canyon, how was he planning on accomplishing that? He couldn't very well maneuver a herd of horses through that type of terrain and fend off a tribe of enraged Lakota at the same time. Such an attempt would be nothing short of suicide. Then, he would be lumped into that category of men who had tried to take the horses and never returned. He would be part of that failed legend. He preferred to stay out of that group.

He remembered one of the two men he had talked to from the saloon, Ted, had mentioned Hangman's Gulch, but the name of the place didn't really help him, either, although he had vaguely heard about it before. It was a place notorious enough that everyone had heard of it.

Hangman's Gulch had a reputation for being notoriously dangerous. Some mistakenly thought the name originated from the idea of people being hanged there, but that was only half of the story behind the name. Hangman's Gulch was a vicious place in the territory, a wild, almost uninhabitable place where the terrain and the surroundings were so untamed and dangerous that people often got disoriented and lost to the point that they hanged themselves from madness and desperation, or so the rumors swirled. He had no idea how much validity could be given to such claims. Whether or not that part of its lore was accurate was something he had no interest in finding out. If people were routinely being hanged there, it made no difference to him why. It was enough that it happened.

But the real reason behind Hangman Gulch's name was because people who wandered there, unwanted people, were hanged as a warning to others who might try to venture there, to stay away. It was a deterrent that some chose to dismiss, but no one was willing to go there to prove it false for themselves. Unfortunately, if his directions were right, it meant you had to pass through Hangman's Gulch in order to make it to this alleged canyon. The other alternative was to travel an even greater distance within Lakota Territory and be subject to their wrath for longer, something that he was simply not interested in trying.

Will sidelined worrying about Hangman's Gulch for the moment and focused his thoughts on the supposed canyon full of horses. There was no need to worry about that part of the trip getting there if there was no 'there' to go to. The whole notion of a canyon remaining full of wild horses just sitting there for the taking was certainly appealing, especially for a man in his desperate situation. But what he would have to go through in order just to find out if it were true wasn't worst dying over. He had to keep reminding himself that if it did exist, there was a valid reason why no one had brought the horses out of there before now.

But while his safety was of the utmost importance to him, he also thought about the practical side of it. Wild horses wouldn't be abandoned by the Lakota, or any other tribe, for that matter, so technically they belonged to no one and taking them wouldn't be stealing because they weren't theirs to begin with. But convincing the Lakota of that would be a problem, since they firmly believed it to be true.

As he made it up to the ranch, he sat briefly in his saddle and looked it over, wondering how much longer he could stay and keep things together. Soon, the bank would be forcing him out of his home and all of this would be taken from him and he would be driven out into the unknown. He could cut and run, leaving a trail of angry creditors in his wake, but that wasn't the right thing to do.

He had no idea where he would end up or what he would do from there. All he did know was that wherever his life took him, it couldn't be here. It was a sad end to a difficult story that he had never seen coming. He had known that ranching was a gamble, and that there were no guarantees, but he never imagined it would have ended up like this, with him basically having to start over with nothing. *All of that time and effort for nothing.*

Harland Fowler had told him that he had a little less than three weeks to try to rectify the situation, but it might as well have been three hours because he couldn't see that anything was going to change in that amount of time. In fact, even giving him two months wouldn't have made any difference. It was what it was, and the odds and the circumstances were stacked against him. He was going to lose his ranch, and it looked like there was nothing he could do to stop it.

Will began wandering through the house, gathering the few things he could take with him and put them in his saddlebags. It suddenly became clear to him what little had remained that he had not sold off to keep hold of the ranch, a realization that troubled him. The sooner he accepted his fate, the better off he would be. The cattle could manage on their own until he got back, or the ranch was sold, whichever one came first, so they weren't a concern. Other than that, there was nothing that required his immediate attention before it was all sold off in a little more than two weeks.

Two weeks.

The deadline lingered in his mind. That didn't give him much time, especially when he wasn't even sure what he was going to do. Could he try to come up with a new plan to save the place? It was highly unlikely or else he would have already come up with such a plan before things had gotten this far out of hand.

There was no one to borrow the money from, not that he would ever have the ability to repay someone, even if he did. Selling off the herd was only a temporary solution, and since they were the biggest part of his investment, it would make no sense to sell off his one main asset. No, that wasn't an option, either.

He faced the haunting truth that he had exhausted all of his other resources. The help would have to come from somewhere else. Things had changed, and now he had been left with no other choice. His mind was made up. He had been backed into a corner and left with no other choices, so that left only one thing he could do.

He had to get those horses.

CHAPTER FIVE

That night's sleep was even more pitiful than usual. It was the intrigue of the story of the trapped horses that he couldn't seem to let go of.

All night long, he had dreamed of finding the horses and then, just as quickly, of being ambushed and massacred by the Lakota. It had seemed so real it had actually startled him awake and prevented him from going back to sleep.

The sun was just skimming the horizon when he finally gave up and got up and got dressed. As he gathered the last of his possessions that he could carry and collected his small stash of money, he considered his next move.

He had left a note on his front door for Harland Fowler, letting him know that he was taking a short trip and if he failed to return by the time the bank was ready to foreclose, the remainder of his cattle were to be sold off and the proceeds given to the owner of the mercantile store, Jack, to settle his bill. If, by some miracle, there happened to be residual money left over, the rest was to be held for him until he returned, whenever that would be. He wasn't betting on the latter as long as Emery Chastain at the land office was involved. He would see that his office and the bank divvied up whatever remained of his ranch.

Initially, he had worried about someone trying to steal his cattle before his return, so he had made sure no one knew of his leaving. The few remaining cattle to his name could graze until his return. If he didn't return, it wouldn't matter anyway and since he had no other kin, his estate would be absorbed by the town, meaning the bank.

Hangman's Gulch was at least a four day ride from there, and that was if he didn't run into any problems, such as being ambushed or even killed along the way, which was not a far stretch when he considered the type of country he would have to pass through just to get there. That would give him maybe five days to travel there, worst-case scenario, a day to gather the horses and another six to make the return. That would be cutting it close. A little too close.

While he wasn't looking forward to confronting the Lakota, there was a more immediate concern swirling around in his mind. The land around Hangman's Gulch was notorious for being the hangout of thieves, killers and other scum of the earth wanted by the law. It was a gathering of the rejects of society that preyed on the weak, those who were unable to protect themselves and those who could be persuaded to do what was demanded of them. It was a place that any sane person would never even consider subjecting themselves to voluntarily and yet, here he was contemplating just that.

That was the other reason why no one had ever successfully found the canyon of horses, he imagined, because they would have to cross through some of the roughest and deadliest area anywhere in the territory. Only a fool would attempt such a feat. A fool or someone who had nothing left to lose and didn't fear death. Given his circumstances, he was pretty sure that he fit both groups.

Like anyone else from around there, he had heard plenty of stories about those who wandered into Hangman's Gulch, stories that could easily be authenticated. The outlaws who inhabited it knew it was a perfect hideout. They knew that their sanctuary was well-guarded because not even the bravest of lawmen would ever attempt to venture there to bring back an outlaw. It would take a posse of considerable size and resources to clean out the area. Even then, without having an accurate count of how many outlaws camped there, they could be hopelessly outnumbered and outgunned, and there would be no way to know if everyone had been cleaned out. Not to mention the problem of being unfamiliar with the terrain and the endless passages and trails that were intertwined within there. It was said to be easy to get turned around in there once you were inside. A posse would be walking into a trap, one that most or none of them would be guaranteed never to come back from. That alone made Hangman's Gulch worth being concerned about.

He needed those horses, but he didn't want to walk into a situation where he was guaranteed to be killed before he even had a chance to get his hands on them. He needed an advantage, some type of edge that would put the odds more into his favor since any type of edge could mean the difference in him making it out of there, alive or not. But what could that edge be? He had to give that some thought.

He considered his chances with the Lakota. There had to be elder natives that had been caught up in the tribe that were inhabiting the valley when the white man had moved in. Most of the tribes were dispersed or relocated and kept as the remnants of a tribe, but there were a few who had chosen to give up resisting and had adapted the white man's ways. Most had accepted the white man's homes, their clothing and their way of life, but that had been years before and most of them had died off, although there was a chance that some had remained. If there were some still living, they could possibly know about Hangman's Gulch and how to get around it. The problem was convincing the Lakota to help him. When it had nothing to do with them. An impossible task, he felt.

Until now, the inhabitants of Hangman's Gulch had not dared challenge the Lakota, and the Lakota had no reason to challenge the outlaws. One of those elders would likely know something about the canyon of horses, but they would never consider discussing it with him. He had to find some other way to get more information.

As he pulled away from the ranch, he stopped and took one final look around, taking in the results of his labor with a saddened heart. It occurred to him that this could be the last time he had the chance to see the place that he called his home. Even if by some miracle he succeeded in bringing back the horses, there would be nowhere to bring them back to if he ran into trouble and went past the due date for the bank to foreclose. Then there was the possibility that he didn't even make it back because of the Lakota, those who were hiding out in Hangman's Gulch, or some other catastrophe, in which case it didn't matter if he came back.

Riding along, he pondered how he had gotten himself into such a predicament. His life had unraveled faster than he could have ever expected. He had known ranching was a risk before he even started, but he had watched as others with less drive and determination had succeeded, so he decided he had it in him to do the same. Then a series of unfortunate incidents had altered his course and, thus, his chance at success, leaving him in a state of desperation. He would never have considered putting his life on the line in such a way before now, but it felt as if he had no other choice, at least none that had presented themselves. It was a sad admission, but if something happened to him, the only ones who would notice this absence were his creditors.

Will Travis was a determined man, a man who had experienced a great deal of setbacks in his short life, but had always managed to pull himself through. But this time was different. Bad weather, coyotes, drought, even rustling, were things he could go up against and come out a survivor. But going up against the bank was different. There was no cheating his way through this.

As he rode, Will reminded himself that he had lived his dream of owning a ranch, even if it had not been successful. That was more than many settlers coming out west could say. He had everything riding on this plan and if it did happen to work out for him, there was nothing that said he couldn't take the money he earned from selling the horses and start over somewhere else, especially now that he knew where he had gone wrong.

At twenty-six years of age, it could be said that he was wise for his years. He was average-size, but solidly built and had never been afraid of hard work. His ranching experience had cut a rough path through him and made him hardened and determined, so if there was any chance of this working, he had the strength and the endurance enough to know that he could make it happen. If not, at least he would die trying. He would need that type of perse-

verance if he was going to see this through to
the end.

He rode off from his ranch, making it a point not
to look back again, the pain of doing so not being
worth what it put him through. His perfect scenario
would be to go straight to the Nakawlee Reservation
and talk to the elders there to inquire about the
canyon of horses, but that was a fantasy. There was
no way anyone was going to divulge any information
about that, especially to him. No, he couldn't rely on
them to offer any help to him and he couldn't say that
he blamed them for it.

There was no one to help. He was going to have
to go about this alone.

It was mid-afternoon by the time Will Travis rode
off towards the direction of Hangman's Gulch. The
thought of venturing into such a place was not at all
appealing to him, nor would it be for anyone else, but
it was all he had to go on and it was the best shot he
had to find the canyon full of horses.

Through the years, he had heard stories of Hangman's Gulch, stories that never had a happy ending
and, more often than not, usually ended with
someone dying or coming up missing. As outrageous
as some of the stories were, he knew them to be true
because they had been verified numerous times by
those who were fortunate enough to escape or who
knew someone who had. So he knew what he was
getting into before he even set out. Still, knowing
what to expect ahead of time was the disturbing part.

Though the straightest route to the canyon was through it, he could still travel around Hangman's Gulch, but that posed its own problem. The only way around it was to pass straight through more Lakota territory, something that he didn't relish thinking about because of the tension between the Lakota and the white settlers. The Lakota had been uprooted from part of their land and seen their treaties broken more than once. They would not be understanding, they would not be helpful, and they certainly would not be merciful.

If he traveled through Hangman's Gulch, he would not be forced to go right through the middle of Lakota Territory, and it would save him time. At least if he opted to travel through Hangman's Gulch, he only had to go through a small portion of the Lakota's land. Either way, there was no sneaking past the tribes, and if he were caught on Lakota land, it would be the end of him in an assuredly unpleasant manner.

He could ask the Lakota for their permission to travel through, but that wasn't a good idea, either. He couldn't very well tell them why he needed safe passage and there was no other legitimate reason for him to do so, at least not one that they would be willing to accept. Once again, that left him with Hangman's Gulch, at least until a better idea came along, which he didn't see happening.

Will wheeled his horse and started in that direction while he devised a plan. He would run into men before making it through the gulch, that was for certain, and when he did, he needed to have a reason to be there, one that they would be more likely to believe. If he didn't, they would rob and kill him, take his gear, and no one would ever be the wiser. It would be as if he simply vanished, like others who had become part of the legend. These men were not easily fooled and had no tolerance for outsiders. They would be looking for a fight, and even if he denied them the opportunity, they would likely press the issue until he conceded.

It was going to be a tricky and dangerous venture, but one that he had to take. If, at any time, he were caught, they would question him. If they felt he was not being honest with them about his presence there, it would all be over in an instant.

None of his options sounded appealing.

CHAPTER SIX

Will's first two days and nights out were uneventful. On the third night, he camped at Stearn's Bluff, where the land began to roughen and become more desolate, giving him a small taste of what lay ahead.

That night was quiet, except for a pair of coyotes whose empty stomachs brought them a little closer to Will's campfire than he was comfortable with, more driven by hunger than by the fear of a man, he thought to himself. His initial sighting of them was startling. He had never seen a coyote so brazen as to approach a man's campfire. Deeper into the night, he had been awakened by the faint stirrings of one of the pair a little too close to his fire and his limited supply of food. Their stirrings kept him from falling victim to their aggression, his curse of being a light sleeper finally paying off for once.

He slept little that night as he was more focused on keeping the coyotes from attacking the buckskin than getting rest. Though he had never heard of a pair of coyotes taking on a horse, he understood that hunger forced creatures to do things and take chances they would otherwise never consider doing. He felt better staying up the remainder of the night and keeping a watch on the buckskin, just in case the coyotes decided it was worth the gamble.

On the morning of the fourth day, he began stirring early before daybreak and ate while surveying the land before him. Exhausted from his scant episodes of sporadic sleep, he had looked around his camp and saw the pair of footprints from the coyotes. He sat on his heels as he studied their movements. What he saw was alarming. The pair had come dangerously close to the fire, and him. *Was this a taste of what he had to expect on this trip?*

The morning chill had been slow to leave and his early coffee was having to work extra to take away the bite in the air, and his exhaustion. He was getting close to Hangman's Gulch, exactly how close he wasn't for certain, but his instincts told him it couldn't be far.

He finished preparing his food as he found it harder to dismiss an unsettling feeling that had begun to creep over him. It was nothing obvious that he could put his finger on, but more of a sensation than anything. He tried to dismiss it, but it lingered still. He also wasn't sure if the chill he felt running down the back of his neck was warranted because of the cooler weather as he ventured closer to the hills or if it were a just anticipation of what was to come. Either way, it was unwanted and uncomfortable.

Once, while saddling the buckskin, he felt as if someone were watching him. He stalled his actions and waited, his senses keen to picking up anything out of the ordinary. He waited, the anticipation almost getting the best of him, which he chastised himself for allowing to happen. The buckskin's ears pricked once and then again a moment later, heightening his awareness even more. He slowly slid his hand down and released his trigger guard as he waited, just to be ready. But after almost a full minute of silence without incident or seeing anything or anyone, and without further reaction from the buckskin, he somewhat relaxed his stance and went back to breaking down his camp so he could be on his way.

He climbed into the saddle, taking time to check his trigger guard to make sure it was off, and loosened the Colt in its holster before urging the buckskin into motion. He hated that he had not slept well the night before, of all nights for that to happen, because whatever happened today would likely be swift and dangerous, and he would have to be on guard for anything. He felt somewhat sluggish, but hoped the cooler air and the constant sun climbing through the sky would revive and boost his attention.

He rode on, the day passing at what seemed like a snail's pace. He had encountered no one since having left the ranch, which he had originally thought to be odd, but when he considered where he was traveling, he convinced himself that it wasn't anything out of the ordinary. But those assurances did little to put him at ease. Every movement, every sound piqued his attention and caused him uneasiness. *Get a grip, Will. It's just your imagination*, he tried to tell himself. *You're just jumpy because of where you're heading, that's all.* But try as he may, he wasn't convincing himself.

The terrain was hardening as more hills exposed the rough terrain just beyond them. The land was unyielding and trails were becoming scarce. He could see the hills transforming into mountains just ahead of him, but still far enough off in the distance not to concern him just yet. He would eventually have to traverse them, one way or another and, more importantly, find a path that would allow him to bring horses back through. Did such a trail exist?

After traveling several hours more, Will topped a ridge and found himself looking down at two small shacks off in the distance. Trading post. Probably the last one before entering the rugged terrain that lay just beyond the hills. The outside of the larger of the two shacks were strewn with animal pelts and other odds and ends, and there was a small corral out in back, no doubt for horses that were for sale or trade. That would be the trading post itself. Judging from the continual plume of smoke rising from the second shack, he took it to be a smokehouse of some kind.

Will eased the buckskin closer. He had gotten his supplies in Liberty before leaving, but there could still be something here that would serve him well that he might have forgotten. If so, he would dip into his reserve money, if needed. It might be the last time he was able to spend it. He would give the place a quick glance and be on his way.

There were two saddled horses tied off out front with no riders visible. He assumed they were probably trappers doing business. There would be no reason for drifters to come this far out of the territory. This was clearly a trading spot and probably the last place before venturing into Hangman's Gulch for anyone to get supplies and information. He urged the buckskin on, keeping a leery eye out for those who would also be there.

Trading posts were often a risk because of the type of individuals who frequented them. While some were honest men plying their trade in order to make a living, these types of men were few and far between in these parts. The other type of individuals who conducted business there did so because they preferred to be left alone. They had shunned society and its advances for a quieter, peaceful existence, earning money through fur trading that got them their bare essentials and nothing more. They lived off the land, required nothing of modern ingenuity, and were content being alone and isolated. These men preferred to be left alone as if they were forgotten, and it was best for men to honor that request.

But there was another group of men found in places such as this. These were trying to stay out of the public eye, meaning staying away from the authorities. These men were wanted by the law for one reason or another and traded their goods in places like this so as to avoid having to venture into town and, subsequently, risk being recognized. They traded here because no one would dare question who they were. They were the type of men who refrained from going into town for those reasons. They were unpredictable and often dangerous. These were the type that he needed to be on the lookout for. Because of that, it would be in his best interest to be extra leery of whoever was in there.

He pulled up out in front and of the actual trading post and tied off his horse. Just before he made his way to the front door, it opened and two men came out, one staggering from having a little too much to drink while the second man, who was not that far behind his friend in being intoxicated, walked beside him and tried to steady the man as best he could. Trying to help his friend proved to be too much for him and the more drunk of the two men staggered and ran his shoulder into Will, the impact causing him to turn and face him with a belligerent stare.

"Why don't you watch where you're going?" The drunkard exclaimed through liquor-soaked breath, as he attempted to stare Will down. When Will tried to ignore him and started again for the door, the drunkard reached out and grabbed Will's arm. "Hey, I'm talking to you, mister," he stated in a slurred manner. "Don't just try to walk away from me when I'm talking to you."

"C'mon, Luther," the second man spoke as he tried to direct his intoxicated friend away from the ruckus and towards their horses. "He ain't worth it," he added as he stole a glance at Will, but the drunk man named Luther would not cooperate and he grabbed at Will's arm a second time before he could be pulled away. Will looked down at the man's grip on his sleeve with annoyance.

"You'd better listen to your friend," Will warned with an icy composure as he stared back at the man. He waited, staring him down, until the man released the grip on his arm before he started for the door. He was turning away from the two men to step inside just as Luther swung.

Will saw the swing coming and easily moved out of the way as Luther felt nothing but air. Will swung a hard right that struck Luther square on the jaw and sent him reeling backwards onto the wooden porch with a thud. The second man, the more sober of the two, came to his friend's defense and reacted by stepping in and trying to hit Will, but Will had anticipated him doing so and ducked far enough out of the way for the man to miss. He quickly followed it with a left to the man's midsection and then a sharp right to the side of his face and then another crashing left that caused the man's knees to buckle as he fell straight down onto the floor next to where Luther was still laying. Will stood his ground and assessed the threat of the two men, neither of whom appeared to be in any condition to stand.

He stepped over the second man and walked inside, catching the attention of the man behind the counter, who had obviously overheard the exchange, but had decided it was something he didn't wish to get involved in. Will caught the man's eyes and then went about picking up some jerky and coffee while the man said nothing.

After glancing around and finding nothing else of need, he walked the items over to the counter. He glanced out the front window to check on his attackers and saw the second man slowly helping Luther up from off of the ground. In protest, Luther snatched his arm away from the man and cut his eyes in through the window directly at Will while the other man retrieved Luther's hat. Will saw them exchange comments, no doubt about him and what had just happened, and then watched as the two men clumsily climbed into their saddles, rubbing their faces in the process and turned their horses west, their hateful, darting glances the last thing he saw as they rode away.

The man behind the counter also watched their departure before he shot Will a look. "That's two bits," he said flatly as he sized up Will, who was fishing money from his pocket. "Not a good idea to rile Luther and Carl like that," he added as he cut his eyes to him while Will dropped part of the money onto the counter.

"Why not?" Will questioned. "They don't look like anything more than a couple of idiots to me."

"I'm just saying. They're not the type to forgive and forget," the man warned as he picked up the coins. "They hold a grudge and neither one of them can be trusted."

"Then they need to keep their hands to themselves," Will warned as he put down the rest of the coins. "I don't like to be touched."

"I'm just trying to warn you, mister, that's all," the clerk explained while he gathered the remaining money. "Those fellas have got lots of friends around here, none of them good, and they look out for one another. You've likely started something you won't want to get in the middle of."

"I'll deal with anyone who wants to put their hands on me in my own way," Will cautioned the man before changing the subject. "How far to Hangman's Gulch?"

"*Hangman's Gulch?* Now I know you're asking for trouble, mister," the clerk stated with profound interest while shaking his head in protest. "Let me give you a piece of advice and you'd be wise to follow it. You'd be better off staying out of there. You'll find nothing but trouble, if you don't. Trouble you won't know how to get out of."

"I don't have a choice. I have to get over past the Lakota reservation. From what I've been told, that's the best way to do that."

"The only other way is to go up and over through

the mountains," he suggested as he motioned out the window at Will's buckskin, "but I wouldn't wish that on the devil himself. It's brutal land, almost impassable. Too dangerous to try." The man pointed out the window at the buckskin. "You'd never make it on horseback. Too rugged and there aren't enough trails to allow a horse through 'em. What trails are there wouldn't hold a jackrabbit. Your horse would break a leg before you got half a day's ride behind 'ya."

"Then it looks like I'm going to have to go through Hangman's Gulch."

"You don't want to do that either, mister," the clerk warned again, this time leaning onto the counter to make sure he had Will's full attention. "That's not some place you want to be. I'm telling you. I've seen people go in there and never come back. I'm telling you, it's a really bad idea."

"Look, I've got to get to the far side of the Lakota. Now, besides going through the mountains, is Hangman's Gulch the only way to do that or not?"

"Yeah, it's the only way, but if you have to make a choice, then I say you'd be better off taking your chances with the Lakota. At least there's a chance that they won't see you and even if they do, you might get lucky and they might not kill you on sight. I can't say the same for whoever you come across in Hangman's Gulch."

"Wonderful," Will answered with a sarcastic tone. "That sounds encouraging."

"Well, you're not giving yourself many options."

"So how far to Hangman's Gulch?"

The clerk hesitated briefly, as if in disbelief that Will had chosen to make the trip anyway, despite his warnings. He turned and pointed out the window. "Just follow this trail to the left for about another fifteen or so miles and you'll run right into it."

"Any chance of avoiding trouble in Hangman's Gulch or the reservation?" He asked as he picked up his things, but before he could wait for the answer, his attention was instinctively diverted to someone who he had not heard come in. It was an old Indian man who had quietly stepped inside without being noticed. The clerk did not take the time to respond to Will's question, but instead immediately chastised the man's presence, his anger quickly turning on the old man.

"Hey! I thought I told you to stay outside," the clerk snapped. The man's curt tone stopped the old man in his tracks, a somewhat confused and humbled look coming over him. He stood somewhat nervously at the door, not knowing what he should do. His failure to leave and his silence only managed to anger the clerk even more. "I said get out!" The clerk snapped again while pointing outside. Will had already seen enough.

"What's he hurting being in here?" Will asked, his tone sharpening as he glanced over at the old man. "He isn't bothering anyone."

"You don't understand, mister," the clerk started, as his attention went back to Will. "He knows he can't hang around here. I've told him numerous times to stay outside," he argued. "He doesn't have any money. He never buys anything. I don't trust him not to try to take stuff without paying for it."

"Has he ever taken anything?"

"Well, no."

"He sounds harmless to me."

"I don't care if he's harmless! He just hangs around here like he's waiting for a handout!" The clerk yelled before returning to the old man. "Which he ain't gettin'!"

"Maybe he doesn't have anywhere else to go," Will suggested, his patience quickly growing thin with the clerk.

"That's not my problem," the clerk quipped as he turned to face the old man again. "I'm trying to run a business here!" The man argued while staring the old man down.

Will tried to calm himself from the situation. "Maybe he's hungry. Have you ever thought about asking him if he needs something to eat?"

"That's not my problem, either! I don't run this place to give handouts to every sad story that comes through here," the clerk said as he reached under his counter and pulled out a short, thick club, his lips pressed tightly together in anger. He had started taking a step towards the old man when Will grabbed the man by the collar and slammed the side of his face down onto the counter, catching him off guard and causing the clerk to whimper from the move.

The move happened so quickly that it stopped the man's movement before he could resist as Will continued to pin his head down with his forearm.

"Let go of the club. *Now.*" He demanded as he tightened his grip on the man's collar. He heard the sound of the club being dropped onto the floor, but he continued to hold on to the man. "Now, I'm going to let go and you're going to act civilized, you understand? And if you even think about trying to pick up that club again, I'll use it on you."

CHAPTER SEVEN

The clerk nervously nodded without speaking as Will slowly released his hold on the man, allowing him to stand back up. The clerk rubbed his neck and shot a mean-spirited glare at the old man before turning the sour expression back onto Will. He had words for Will, but decided it was best not to say anything.

Will cut the clerk an agitated glare to remind him of his threat before he walked over to the old man, who gently cowered when he came near him, unsure whether Will meant him harm. "It's okay, I'm not going to hurt you," he assured the old man, who seemed to somewhat relax at the comment. Will glanced the man over. He looked to be in his sixties, his face a collection of lines and wear from living a long life in the elements. He stood nearly as tall as Will, yet he could tell the old man weighed almost thirty pounds less. His clothes were weathered and hung loosely on him. Will surmised that it was probably because the old man had not eaten consistently for some time. He also saw no evidence that he had any belongings to speak of. He worried how he would make it through the winter in this territory that was quickly bearing down on them.

"Are you hungry?" Will asked as he shot the clerk a careful glance, as if to ensure the man remembered his warning to him. The clerk rubbed his face in response, but said nothing.

The old man barely made eye contact with Will as he softly and humbly nodded his head in embarrassment.

"Go pick out whatever you want," Will advised him. The old man looked up at Will, his face reflecting the surprise at the offer as if he questioned whether or not Will was telling him the truth. "It's okay," Will assured him again with a reassuring nod as he shot the clerk another determined stare, a stare that also quietly advised the clerk not to intervene. The old man glanced at the clerk, too, waiting for his inevitable resistance. Will picked up on the old man's hesitation.

"He isn't going to say anything," Will assured him as he glanced at the clerk. "Are you?" He stated more as a point than a question. He could tell the clerk wanted to say something about him helping the old man, but he feared Will's reaction more than he cared to voice his opinion. Both men waited as the clerk slowly shook his head.

The old man slowly walked over to where the

jerky and other food items were and carefully chose a few things. Will saw the old man's hesitance and walked over to him and picked up several more packages of jerky and some other things that he thought the old man might want, and piled them in his arms. He then walked with him up to the counter where Will stood next to him and nodded that it was still okay for him to do so as the old man dumped his goods on the counter.

"You start buying him stuff and he'll never leave," the clerk warned, his mouth clamped tightly in disgust and quiet protest.

"Can't you see the man is hungry? Are you going to deny someone food just because of who they are?"

The clerk gave him a foul look, his face hurting as bad as his pride. "I ain't no charity, mister."

"He isn't. *I'm* paying."

"But you won't be here the next time he comes in here begging for a handout."

"Then maybe he could sweep or do something to help you clean up around this pigpen."

"I just don't want him around here, that's all."

Will could see he would get nowhere with the man's attitude. "Just add it up," a thoroughly disgusted Will spoke sternly as he fished more money from his pocket. He was quickly losing patience with the man, and it was taking all of his resolve not to pull him over the counter and beat him senseless.

"That'll be six bits," the clerk announced as he cut another cross glance at the old man who was humbly standing next to Will, but slightly behind him. It was when Will glanced over at the old man that he noticed he was softly shivering. Will turned and picked up a blanket from off a table behind them and tossed it onto the counter. "This, too."

The clerk flashed a disgusted look. "You sure you want to go to all this trouble, mister? Y'know, he ain't your responsibility..."

"I'm sure. Add it up."

The clerk scoffed in disgust. "That'll cost you another *three* dollars," the clerk said in a appalled tone, making sure to point out to Will how much he was going to be spending on the old man.

Will dropped the coins on the counter and picked up the items, handing them to the old man without speaking. He shot the clerk one last disgusted stare before he walked to the door, with the old man following behind him.

Will stepped outside of the trading post as he took a look around him. The landscape of the country was getting harsh and soon he would have to make the choice of if he would go through Hangman's Gulch or try to go around it and take his chances in the mountains, even as treacherous as they sounded.

He wondered how difficult a time the buckskin was going to have if he stayed off of Lakota land and chose to travel around Hangman's Gulch. If it was as dangerous as they said, he would never be able to drive a herd of horses through it on his return, but maybe he could use it as a way to get there only. Either way, he wasn't looking forward to the trip. He glanced over at the old man, who appeared to be lost as to where to go.

"Do you have a place to stay?" Will asked with concern. Being this close to the mountains was a concern. Once the sun went down, it was going to be cold and the old man didn't look like he had much resources available to him. The old man coughed deeply and remained quiet as he shook his head gently.

"Then come with me," Will advised him. "You can share my camp."

After tying the old man's things onto the buckskin, they set out. He heard the old man cough again. It felt awkward to ride when the old man would be forced to walk so Will decided to let him ride the buckskin off into the direction of the hills while still keeping an eye out for the two men he had encountered, just in case they developed a burst of courage and came back to try their luck at him again. He trusted the old man, but chose to hold on to the reins, just in case his judgement was clouded.

They traveled for several miles until Will felt satisfied that they were far enough away from the trading post to not be seen. He fashioned a ring of rocks close to the base of the rock face and had a fire going in the middle of it in no time while the old man sat next to the building flame with his blanket wrapped around him to fend off the advancing cool of the coming evening. Will wandered off and returned a short time later with a rabbit he had shot. He had cleaned it and was lying against the underside of his saddle watching it on the spit, lost in his thoughts.

"Kawnteenowah," the old man said, speaking for the first time, instantly drawing Will's attention from the flames of the fire and causing him to look over at him. The old man began coughing deeply from within. Will scoffed softly while flashing a faint smile. He had begun to think the old man could not speak.

"Well, you rascal. So you *can* talk," Will pointed out with a snicker. "You just didn't want to, did you? I don't blame you. That idiot of a clerk wasn't worth wasting words on."

"Kawnteenowah," the old man repeated.

"Con-tee-no-wah," Will pronounced the word slowly. "What is that? Is that your name?"

"You seek valley of horses," the old man clarified, still staring into the fire. "Kawnteenowah."

Will sat speechless, unsure as to what to say as he looked past the fire to the old man. "How do you know about that?" He asked curiously. "I never mentioned it around you where I was headed."

"You go Hangman's Gulch. Bad land. Not good place. Heard you ask man at trading post about it. He not like me," the old man's indifferent voice trailed off after the admission.

"What's your name?" Will asked.

"I am Walks With Horse."

"Will Travis," Will responded while touching his chest. "What does Hangman's Gulch have to do with this valley of horses, this Kawnteenowah, as you call it?"

"Kawnteenowah on Lakota land. Must go through bad land to get to Lakota land. Only reason man go through bad gulch and onto Lakota land is to look for Kawnteenowah. Bad idea. You not first white man to look for valley," the old man said as he coughed again. "Many try before and no come back. Many dead." Walks With Horse coughed.

Will took notice of the old man's nagging cough. "Are you alright?"

"Yes. My strength leaves me. I go to spirit world soon."

Will looked confused at the admission. "Can your Lakota medicine not help you?"

"Nothing help Walks With Horse now."

"If your medicine can't help you, aren't you at least going to try something else? Can not the white man's medicine help you?"

"No need. I am Lakota brave. I have fought many battles and ready to die in all of them. Walks With Horse not afraid of death."

Will decided it best to change the subject. "You speak pretty good english," he said with surprise.

"If live with white man, must learn white man words," the old man stated with assurance.

Will's curiosity got the better of him as he sat up. "How do you know about this valley of horses? I heard it was just a legend. So you're saying the legend is true? That it really does exist?"

"You seek what you cannot have, Travis," Walks With Horse continued as he stared into the fire. "White man not welcome in valley. Only Lakota."

"So it *does* exist," he stated assuredly.

The old man looked at Will and nodded softly. "Yes," he reluctantly answered as he stared back into the fire.

"Where did it come from?" Will asked as his interest peaked. "I mean, the horses. Who put them there?"

"Legend says valley made by ancient ones," he started. "Horses live there to carry brave warriors who have died with honor off into spirit world."

Will gave him a skeptical look. "You know your ancestors didn't put those horses there, don't you?"

"That is what you believe. Does not matter what white man thinks. It is what we believe. But horses not for white man to take."

"How many horses are we talking?"

"Don't know," Walks With Horse answered. "But white man cannot have. Only braves to have horses."

"I'm not trying to be greedy. I don't need all of them," Will responded. "I only want a few."

"You not go into valley, Travis. Bad medicine in Kawnteenowah. Bad medicine for any white man. You go there, you die."

"You don't understand," Will stated. "I need those horses. I'm about to lose everything I own. I don't have a choice. I have to get them back so I can sell them."

"Money not worth dying."

"I have to. I don't have any other choice."

"Always have choice, Travis," the old man said matter-of-factly. "Do not let horses lead you to death."

Will ignored the warning. "This canyon, this Kawnteenowah. You say it's on Lakota land?"

"Yes, but I warn you. You must not go there, Travis. Lakota not like white man on land. Not like white man in canyon. You will not live."

"I appreciate your concern, but I have to go. If I can bring a few of those horses back, maybe I can still save my ranch. If those are pure, wild stock like you say they are, then I can get upwards of three-hundred dollars a head for them."

"Bad medicine for you, Travis," Walks With Horse said flatly. "You no go, you live."

Will continued to try to reason with Walks With Horse, but the old man would not have any of it. Walks With Horse would not tell him anything else either. Will felt it was more because he was trying to protect him than from just being stubborn. Anytime Will tried to press him for more information, the old man would keep telling him not to go looking for the valley. It was frustrating, but at the same time, he understood the old man's concern.

Finally, he realized Walks With Horse wasn't going to help him anymore, so he decided to drop the subject. They ate in silence, after which Will fed the fire one final time while the old man curled up next to it and coughed deeply before he fell asleep without uttering another word.

For quite some time, Will laid with his eyes open, staring up at the night sky and visualizing the valley of horses. Just the thought of coming across such a sight was exciting to consider. It felt better knowing its existence had been verified by a Lakota. He might not have an exact location for it, but at least he now knew that the legend was true. Now he had to find someone who could lead him the rest of the way, or at least tell him how to get there.

It had been an interesting day, but it had also been a long day and fatigue finally set in enough that he was able to find a less painful position in his bedding and close his eyes. As he drifted off to sleep, he told himself that all he had to do was travel across Hangmans' Gulch, without being shot, and wander onto Lakota land, without being shot, until he found the canyon, or until they spotted him and killed him, whichever came first.

He didn't like his choices.

Will opened his eyes as the first beams of morning filtered over the hillside. When he glanced over to where Walks With Horse had been lying, the old man and the blanket were gone. He checked his saddle-bag, which had been laying close to his own bedding, and found that the items he had bought the old man were also missing, but nothing else. Will scoffed at the old man's ability to move about without being heard, especially by him. How he managed to slip past him in the middle of the night, he had no idea.

He ate and had begun to break down his camp when something caught his attention. He looked over to see a handmade bead necklace hanging from the saddle pommel right above where his head had been while he had slept. He instantly recognized it as one that Walks With Horse had been wearing and decided it must have been the old man's way of paying him back for buying him the blanket, the food and a place to stay for the night. Out of respect for the old man, he slipped the necklace over his neck and, after saddling the buckskin, turned him west towards Hangman's Gulch, Lakota land, and hopefully towards the canyon of horses.

Kawnteenowah.

He ran it over and over through his mind, the name almost haunting him as he rode. His enthusiasm built as he continued on. If everything the old man had said was true, then at least he knew the canyon existed and roughly where it might be, although the Lakota Territory was quite expansive, and just knowing that it was there without having more to go on was rather vague. But that still didn't solve his biggest problem. How was he not only going to slip onto Lakota land undetected, but to also corral and drive a herd of horses out of the canyon without being discovered? It sounded like an impossible task, for sure, but it was one that he had to try, regardless.

The terrain became more intense as he continued on and the landscape began to change to become more challenging. He rode along, his attention focused more on the rising height of the climbing walls around him than anything else. He didn't like feeling pinned in or of having his options limited and this was a perfect example of such. He couldn't shake the thought of a man with a rifle posted up there who could easily take him out or, at the very least, have him at a huge advantage if he wanted and wound him until his friends arrived.

There were high walls of rock on either side of him and the path he was on, an old dried-up riverbed, narrowed and curved back and forth through the disfigured formations so much that he couldn't see very far in front of him, making it virtually impossible to see anyone who might be lying in wait up ahead. Being in such a vulnerable position did not sit well with him. Someone could ambush him before he knew what was happening. The surroundings would be strictly to someone's advantage who wanted to ambush him. He did not like the situation that he had placed himself in. There were simply too many factors against him. If someone did surprise him, he doubted he could get the buckskin turned around and out of sight before he was shot right out of his saddle.

As he rode along, he felt the hair on the back of

his neck stand up and an unsettling feeling overcame him. Was it because of where he was heading into and the stories he had heard about it or was it just his imagination running wild? It wasn't like him to get spooked, but there was something about the high walls on either side of him that he did not like. Normally, riding through such a place wouldn't bother him to this extent, but this place came with a reputation for being violent. But despite his apprehension and edginess and the isolation of the place, the thing that he disliked the most was that it was quiet.

A little too quiet.

CHAPTER EIGHT

Will had not wanted to travel through Hangman's Gulch, but considering the other options, he felt as if he had no other choice. The thought of risking the buckskin's life on those treacherous trails was more than he was willing to bet on.

To the west of it was a vast series of canyons, most too deep and too rugged to get through without considerable effort, and even then the going was questionable, at best. He trusted the buckskin to endure such hazardous terrain, but he also didn't want to put it in that type of unnecessary danger. The buckskin's dedication was such that it would go wherever he led it without question and without hesitation. But the going would be slow, painfully slow, if he wanted to be careful. He didn't have that kind of time and, as strong as the buckskin was, he wasn't convinced the horse could make it through them, anyway.

To the north was open prairie, but no water for days, something that he could not even consider trying to get through with a herd of horses. Horses would become stressed if they had to go without water for more than a day, especially if there were foals in the midst. He couldn't risk doing that to them and it wasn't the humane thing to do, anyway. That left only Hangman's Gulch. And whoever occupied it knew it.

He adjusted the Colt again in its holster, letting his uneasiness and his imagination get the better of him as he kept his eyes on the rock walls above him on either side.

He cursed under his breath at his uneasiness and for being there all alone, out in the open and making himself an easy target like this. All he could focus on was how it was the perfect place for an ambush. By the time he could react to being fired upon and try to return fire, he would first have to find the shooter and then draw them out from the rocks enough for him to get in a clear shot. Looking up into the bright sunlight would make that difficult- very difficult. By the time all that transpired, it would all be over with. That was reason enough that he had to pay attention. There was no room for error or bad judgement here. Not if he wanted to live.

He had weaved his way around the trail for quite a while without incident, but he still wasn't convinced he was alone.

Something was off.

His instincts were kicking in. His edginess was through the roof. He had no real proof of his suspicions, just that every little sound felt like it was amplified. He tried to make very little sound, but there was a minimal amount generated from a walking horse that couldn't be helped. It was nothing out of the ordinary, just the usuals sounds of being alone out in the hills. But that did very little to console him. He couldn't put his finger on the issue that was bothering him just under his skin, but it was almost as if he could sense it before he saw it.

Twice, he thought he caught a glimpse of someone on the top of the rock walls, but both times it was only for a split second and then there was no one. *Had he imagined it? Possibly. Had his imagination created such a threat? If someone were up there stalking him, why had they not acted on it? What were they waiting for? For him to get deeper in their encampment? Was it the sun playing tricks on him? Or was it just his edginess getting the better of him?* He hoped that was all it was.

He continued on, glancing down at the trail in between stealing glances up at the rock walls on either side. The trail was a dried creek bed that had not seen a regular current in some time, but that didn't mean it should be ignored. These small trails were notorious for flash floods. The narrow trail combined with the high walls worked as a funnel that could bring the level of the water up to a horse's neck without warning.

He looked over the creek bed looking for signs of

horses, but the ground was too parched and the small rocks lining the bottom were hiding any signs of recent movement very well. At least for now, he would have to rely just on what he saw.

Suddenly, he caught a glimpse of movement off to his right. He drew his gun before he realized it and whirled it around without giving it thought as a jackrabbit hopped out in front of him, obviously as startled at Will's presence there as he was of it, giving him a curious stare before it casually hopped away around a cluster of boulders. Will shook off the surprise with a deep exhale as he holstered his gun, taking in a deep breath, trying to shake the tension out of his reflexes.

Will was looking for a place to stop and give the buckskin a rest when he saw him, a man dodging his sight and making his way across the top of the wall on his right, with a rifle in hand. It was just a glimpse for a split-second, but it was enough for him to know that it was real.

The man appeared and then disappeared several times as he used various rocks for cover while he moved farther down the wall. He must have realized that his cover was blown, for he didn't appear to be trying to hide it any longer. If he had been spotted, turning and making a run for it wouldn't matter at this point.

Will instinctively pulled and cocked the Colt and quickly paused the horse's erratic movements. The animal stomped in place nervously, picking up on

Will's interest in what was stalking them and mixing
it with its own uneasiness. He pulled back on the
reins in an attempt to quell the horse's anxiousness,
yet he was still having trouble settling the animal
down, more than he ever had before. Whatever he
was anticipating was being picked up by her horse
and was spooking him as well.

He continued scanning the walls for others, his
gun drawn and ready, but, so far, it had just been the
one man that he had seen. But that meant nothing to
him. This was Hangman's Gulch. Where there was
one, there were sure to be others.

The buckskin was becoming increasingly agitated
as it snorted its discontent, moving back and forth in
half-circles as it picked up on Will's jitters. It wanted
to leave this place, leave it now. If he kicked at the
horse to run, it would surely go barreling back in the
direction they had just come. He wrestled with the
horse's nervousness while he tried to remain focused
on the spot on the wall where he had last seen the
man disappear but, for some reason, the man had not
reappeared.

He considered his options. Trying to make a run
for it now would be nothing short of foolish.
Whoever was up there knew he was there. As soon as
his back was turned to try to leave, the man could put
a bullet in him or shoot the buckskin out from
beneath him. He wasn't showing them his back. He
would face them, whoever they were, head-on. There
would be no running away from it now. Whenever

they wanted, they would gun him down before he even made it to the first corner.

Sweat ran down his temples as his eyes strained to see past the glare of the bright-colored rock high up on the top of the walls, but so far there had been no other movements. Where had the man gone and why hadn't anyone else shown themselves? He cursed under his breath at putting himself in such a predicament, regretting being there at all. Without being able to see any of them, it was their decision when he would be confronted. As much as he hated the notion, he would have to wait for them to make the first move. He continued to scan the walls.

He waited.

"Rider! Drop your gun!" a voice called out from another spot on the opposite wall, snapping Will's attention over in that direction. His gun was ready for what it was worth, but there was no target. He felt like a fool. There were undoubtedly numerous guns on him or the individual would not have given away his position. Surely there had to be a way out of this, but if there was, he didn't know what that could be and he was afraid to try anything bold for fear of being cut down before he could act.

"I said drop your gun!" the man repeated, this time louder.

Will paused, hoping the man would show himself so he could get a better shot. He wouldn't shoot first, but he was certainly ready to defend himself.

"Don't be a damn fool, mister. I know what you're

thinking and I'm telling you right now that it ain't gonna work," the stranger's voice added. "You don't stand a chance and you know it. You'd just be getting yourself killed for nothing. Is that what you want?"

Will remained silent, his thoughts racing through his head as he sought a way out. He could hear the impatience in the man's voice the next time he spoke.

"I know you can hear me! Not saying anything tells he you aren't willing to cooperate, and that's only going to get you shot. We've got you covered, no matter which way you try to go. Now drop it or we drop you!"

Will ran his only options through his mind. If he kept his weapon, he had at least a slight chance of escaping, but if he was unarmed, he had no chance at all and he would be at their mercy.

He hesitated.

"First, you need to step out into the open!" he demanded. I want to see who I'm talking to!" He responded as he fought with the reins to quell the buckskin's growing uneasiness.

"You don't get to make the rules!" The man responded, this time with building anger and impatience in his voice. "I call the shots and I've got a half-dozen rifles on you right now, so don't try to be a hero. You so much as blink too hard and you're a dead man!"

"How do I know you won't shoot me, anyway?" Will asked.

"You don't, but if I wanted you dead, trust me,

you'd already be dead!" The man called out. "Now I'm not going to tell you again to drop your gun!"

Will hesitated to respond when a bullet kicked dirt up next to the buckskin's feet, startling the already spooked horse and causing him to buck. What was troubling was that the shot had originated from behind him, in a different direction than either the man speaking or the man he had witnessed scaling the top of the wall. It was a show of force. That meant there were at least three of them- at least. The bad part was he had no idea how many he was going up against. The man was right. They had the drop on him and would likely cut him down before he got off more than a single shot.

"The next one goes in you!" The man yelled. "Now drop that gun! Do it now!"

Feeling defeated and outgunned, Will complied and released the hammer before replacing his revolver and unbuckling his gun belt, throwing it into the dirt. "The rifle, too!" The man demanded, causing Will to reach for it, but the man obviously thought Will was moving too quickly. "Nice and slow, mister!"

Will stopped briefly and then slowly continued to pull it from its scabbard and toss it down as well as he raised his hands. A few seconds later, a man appeared from the bottom of the wall on the left while four more came up from behind him and the man he had originally seen on the top of the rock wall also came into view from his perch. Each of the men was holding their guns pointed at him.

"How's it look, Dobbs?" shouted the man who had been talking to the man who remained on top of the rock wall.

"He's alone," the man called Dobbs responded after one last confirming glance.

The man in front of him and on his left walked closer, stopping some twenty feet away from the buckskin. "So you're alone, huh? We don't get many visitors in here, mister, so you're either crazy or just plain stupid for coming in here like this," the man announced with a soft grin as he scanned the faces of his colleagues, his gun still pointed at Will. "Or maybe you're like us and you're wanted by the law," he added. "Which one is it?"

"I just wanted to pass through," Will tried explaining. "I'm not here to cause trouble."

"Well, now you see, mister, that's a bit of a problem," the man continued. "Y'see, this here is *our* hideout and we don't take kindly to strangers wandering in, now do we fellas?" He stated as he once again looked at them for their reaction. "Besides, it ain't just me that you gotta answer to. There's others in this gulch. Others just like us and they ain't as friendly and welcoming as we are. They don't take too kindly to strangers coming in here, either. But they ain't like us. They're liable to shoot first and ask questions later. You're better off to have run across us first instead of them. Hell, mister," he said with a sarcastic smile and tone, "we might have just saved your life."

Will scanned the faces of those that he could

readily see and none of them appeared to be tolerant of him being there. They were laughing at his expense, but behind their humor, he could tell deep down they resented him being there. The man continued with his line of questioning, still not convinced that Will had ventured there by accident.

"You a lawman?"

"No, I'm no lawman," Will answered, choosing his words wisely. "Like I said, I was just passing through."

"Don't listen to him, Bell," one of the men behind Will offered to the man who was talking. "He wouldn't admit it if he was a lawman."

"Shut up, Harvey," the man in charge, Bell, ordered. "He ain't wearing a badge. Besides, ain't a lawman in the entire territory stupid enough to come in here after us. They know what would happen to 'em." The man called Bell turned to Will. "We've had run-ins with the law before and I got to say, it never turned out good for the lawman."

Several of the men nodded, but the misfit named Harvey would not let go of his hunch. "Just because he ain't got a badge, don't mean he don't have one. He could have taken it off, Bell. I say we search him."

"Shut up, Harvey," the man called Bell berated him again. "I don't think he's a lawman," he stated, as he looked Will over carefully.

"What makes you say that?" Another of the men asked.

"Because he don't carry himself like a lawman," Bell surmised. "He ain't got that high-and-mighty attitude about him like a lawman. He don't look like he answers to anyone, either. Nah, this is just a stupid cowboy who lost his way. Ain't that right, mister stupid cowboy?"

"That's right," Will agreed as he stole a glance at the four men who had walked up from behind him and stood on both sides of his horse, just out of his reach.

Bell looked back his way. "Where you from, mister?"

"Liberty."

"If you're from Liberty, then what are you doing way out here? There's nothing out this way but outlaws and indians. If you came all this way out of your way, you had to have a reason behind it. So what is it?"

"Like I said, I was just passing through."

Bell was growing impatient at the lack of information. "Yeah, you keep saying that, but I've gotta tell you, mister, I don't believe you. People don't just ride all the way out here just to 'pass through'. There's more to your story that you're not telling us."

"I wish there was," Will tried convincing him, "but that's it. I guess I picked the wrong place to go through." He looked at Bell for a reaction, but the man clearly wasn't buying his story.

"What're we gonna do with him, Bell?" A juiced-up Harvey inquired as he flashed an excited grin, his eyes wide with excitement. "We're gonna kill him here and take his horse and guns, ain't we?"

"No. Too messy. Besides, we can't bury him here. Ground's too hard and I don't want to have to carry him out of here. We'll take him back to the camp," Bell stated calmly. "Then, I'll decide what to do with him."

CHAPTER NINE

The man they called Bell led the way as they took a side cut and wandered a way through the maze of trails until they came to a small clearing. Will tried to keep a memory of where they were going in case he got away and had to retrace his tracks to get out of there, but the sheer number of turns and new trails they took were too much to remember.

After some time, they came upon a clearing. There in the middle was a makeshift shack with horses tied off on a picket line and a wagon parked beside it. Two more men were standing next to a fire talking, obviously waiting for Bell and the others to return. They looked up when the group came into view. Will instantly recognized the last two men by the fire as the ones he had gotten into the fight with at the trading post, Luther and Carl. The drunkard of the two, Luther, angrily tossed the remnants of his coffee onto the ground as he stared with hatred at the sudden sight of Will.

"What's *he* doing here?!" Luther demanded as he stomped his way closer to Will.

"You know this guy?" Bell asked with a glance as he holstered his gun.

"That's the man that jumped us at the trading post," Luther confessed as he walked closer to them, his mouth tightening with anger. "He's the one that did this!" He shouted as he pointed to the bruise that had formed on his swollen jaw.

"I didn't jump you," Will declared calmly. "You two losers picked a fight, and you lost."

Luther lunged for Will, but Bell and another man caught him and held him back before he could make it to him. Will was unscathed by the threat and did not move. "Take it easy, Luther!" Bell instructed him. "You're just mad because his answer sounds a little more believable than yours does."

An enraged Luther shook himself free of their grasp and stared Will down. "Look at what he did to me, Bell!" He exclaimed as he pointed angrily to his bruised jaw and bloody cheek. "Are you going to let him get away with this?"

"If you picked a fight with the wrong man, that's your problem, Luther," Bell admitted, downplaying the injuries. "Now take Darius and tend to the horses," Bell said calmly as he started to pour himself a cup of coffee. Luther did not move, but instead stood his ground, the anger welling up inside him as his hatred forced him to continue staring at Will.

"It ain't fair! He needs to pay! Do something, Bell!" Luther demanded, slowly inching his way towards Will.

"Shut up, Luther, and tend to those horses, like I told 'ya," Bell instructed him, but Luther continued glaring at Will. That was when Bell exploded. "I said move!" Bell snapped as he grabbed Luther by the back of the collar and threw him in the direction of the horses, almost causing him to lose his balance and fall. Luther staggered, but regained his footing and continued towards the horses, turning to look back at Will in the process. Bell turned back to Will with a hateful glare.

"Knowing what I know about Luther and his inability to control his drinking, and his mouth, I'm more apt to believe you, mister. But if you try any of that with me, I'll cut you down and never think twice about it. Do you understand?" Right then, a man came up next to him, holding Will's guns. "Put 'em next to the fire," he instructed the man before he turned back to Will again and pointed at him. "You, climb down."

Will complied and stepped down from his horse, making sure to keep an eye on Bell. As Bell turned back towards the campfire, two of the other men silently pointed their rifles in his direction as a way of telling Will to follow him. Satisfied that Luther wasn't going to cause any more trouble, Bell finished pouring his cup of coffee and then turned back to Will. "So, I'm going to ask you again. Who are you? And don't lie to me, mister."

"Like I keep trying to tell you, I'm just passing through," Will said, sticking to his story.

"Yeah, I know that's the story you wan to stick to, but you and I both know that you're lying," Bell declared as he took a cautious sip. "No one just up and wanders through here without a reason. You've got a reason and I want to know what it is, right now."

"I already told you."

Bell looked at one of the men standing behind Will and nodded slightly. The man slammed his rifle butt into the small of Will's back, dropping him to one knee as he grimaced in pain. Bell looked at Will calmly. He already seemed bored with the conversation. "Let's try this again. I ask the questions and you answer them or you get hurt. I'll ask you again. *Why* are you *here?*"

Will struggled to slowly stand again as he fought to catch his breath. "I told you... I'm passing through."

This time, the man who had struck Will hit him in the back of the head with the rifle butt, this time dropping Will all the way onto the ground as if his legs had collapsed.

"I can last a lot longer at this than you can, mister," Bell declared boldly, his tone getting more and more agitated as he casually took a sip of his coffee. "So you'd better start giving me some answers or I can promise you you're going to have a really bad day."

Will fought to raise his head from the dirt, the powdery dust caked onto the side of his sweaty face. He could feel the warmth of fresh blood running down the sides of his neck from where his skull had been split open. He tried to speak, but it took several seconds for his brain to distinguish what he was trying to do.

"Look... I don't know who you are or what you did, and I don't care. You could be wanted by the law, for all I know. I'm telling you the truth," he struggled to say through labored breathing. "You can beat me all day long, but the answer isn't going to change. I'm a drifter."

The man who had struck him stepped in to administer more punishment, but Bell held up his hand to stop him just as the man had pulled the rifle back to hit him again. "Alright. Suppose you are just passing through. Where 'ya headed?"

"I don't really know," Will spilled through heavy breaths. "Wherever the road takes me."

Bell stepped over and grabbed a handful of Will's hair on the back of his head. Blood oozed from between his fingers, but he didn't care, as he violently snatched Will's head up where he was back up on his knees so he could look into his face. Bell leaned down to get closer to him. "I'm running out of patience with you, mister, so you'd better start giving me some answers that I'll believe right now!" He released Will's hair and casually wiped the blood onto the shoulder of Will's shirt as he slowly circled Will, who was still on all fours on the ground, his head now hanging from the pain.

Will struggled to speak. "I... don't know where I'm going. I was... just drifting."

Bell was unamused at the answer and kicked Will hard in the side. The blow forced the air from Will's lungs and caused him to collapse onto the ground as he favored his side and began wheezing as he fought to breathe in. He choked and coughed hoarsely as he tried to inhale.

"Where... were... you... going?" Bell asked again as he continued to slowly circle Will like a predator. Will tried to take in a deep breath, but his breathing was raspy from him, still trying to catch his breath.

"I'm a drifter," was all he could manage to say between wheezes.

By now, Bell had walked around him and kicked violently at his other side. The thud it produced was followed by Will gasping for air and coughing deeply as he labored to regulate his breathing. His breaths had been reduced to hoarse, deep, labored gasps.

"I can promise you that you ain't getting out of here without telling me what I want to know," Bell wanted. "I'm starting to think that maybe you could be a lawman. If you are, I've gotta tell you you're the stupidest one I've ever met."

Will fought for enough breath to speak. "I'm... a lawman."

"Y'know, I think I've figured you out," Bell admitted with a coy smile. "I wondered if you were crazy or stupid for coming here," he stated as he leaned down closer to Will's face and looked him in the eye. "Looks to me like you're both," he added as he gritted his teeth and swung his boot hard, catching Will at the temple and slamming his head over to the side before his body dropped into the dirt as he fell unconscious. Bell stepped back and surveyed the damage he had inflicted, his fury over not receiving answers almost too much for him to control.

"What do we do with him, boss?" One of the men asked as they started gathering around Bell and Will.

"Tie him to the wagon wheel," Bell ordered as he looked back down at Will's motionless body while trying to calm himself down with a deep exhale. "When he wakes up, we'll give him some more beatings. He obviously likes it."

It was well past dark when Will finally began to stir. When he tried to lift his head, his neck felt as if it had been stomped on by his horse. He tried to register where he was, but his brain was in too much of a fog to help him. His head throbbed terribly, worse than he had ever imagined it could, and his eyes took a few minutes of staring before they cooperated enough that he could accurately relay what he was seeing while his memory reminded him of what had happened.

His head hung gently to the side and in an awkward angle, but, strangely, it felt a little better that way. He did not underhand why.

There was a sticky sensation on the lower part of the back of his head and neck and down to his shoulders. When he tried to turn his head, there was a slight bit of resistance. It took him a few minutes before he realized it as a coating of dried blood from his head injury of being struck with the rifle stock.

Will looked around him and saw Bell and his men all sleeping around the campfire. He also noticed that there was no one on guard. So confident was Bell of his hideout that he felt no need to post to a guard.

He tried to move, but the ropes securing him to the wagon wheel prevented him from doing such. He was prevented from doing even the smallest of adjustments. After testing the tension of the ropes more, he found it to be hopeless, and he decided to abandon his efforts and save his energy as much as possible. He would need it later, he reasoned.

Will sat quietly, contemplating his situation. He was thirsty, hungry, cold, and exhausted. The beating had taken it out of him, more than he was willing to admit. He wondered if he would survive the night, if he had it in him to push through the pain, but even that wasn't reassuring. Even if he was able to live till morning, it was of little comfort to him since he doubted if Bell and his men would allow him to make it through the day before he was beaten to death.

Even if he admitted his plans to search for the valley of horses, Bell would likely not believe him, thinking he was just rambling to try to save his hide. They could believe him and demand that he take them with him. But without an accurate location for the valley, Bell would eventually think he was lying and kill him for wasting his time following him.

Even if Bell did believe him, what then? They would extract as much information from him as they could and then kill him when they believed him to be of no further use. Either way, he was as good as dead unless he could come up with a plan. A solid plan.

An impossible plan.

The longer he remained awake, the more he realized that his right arm was noticeably more painful than the left one. He wondered why until he tried to adjust his position and he found out. The rope was twisted around his wrist and was partially cutting off the blood flow to his hand, leaving him with a dull feeling in it. HIs gun hand. The hand he would need should an opportunity present itself. He tried to move it enough to get some relief, but there was no use. It was too tight. Every time he tried to move, it only seemed to tighten more and make matters worse, causing him to eventually abandon his efforts.

He tried to clear his thoughts, but his condition was such that it proved to be more difficult than he imagined. He had slipped in and out of consciousness throughout the afternoon and evening, that much he could remember. Only bits and pieces, really. Other than that, the events since being captured were still a little vague to him.

He was exhausted. *How much more abuse could he take from Bell?* That was unknown. Regardless, he knew he would find out soon enough.

Will laid his head back against the wheel, trying to get as comfortable as possible, but that was a moot point. Sitting up like this had done nothing to help his battered sides, and the pain that Bell and the others had inflicted seemed to be amplified by his position. He tried to take in a deep breath, but between his tortured sides and the restraints of the ropes, he failed to do so.

He closed his eyes again, willing himself to try to get at least some rest, anything that would help him try to recover from his beating as much as he could, and take his mind off of his current situation. But there was no position that would help and without rest and food, he could have no hope of being able to defend himself when they awoke. Besides, there was no going up against seven or eight men, even if he hadn't been severely beaten first. The reality of the situation was that he was growing weaker as time passed, making his resistance that much worse. He began to accept the likelihood that he would prob-ably die before ever seeing the outside of this canyon.

Will had unknowingly dozed off when he was suddenly brought out of a semiconscious state when he felt a hand cover his mouth tightly. The movement shook him from his distorted sleep, the sudden jolt creating a grunt of pain as he frantically opened his eyes to see Walks With Horse squatting in front of him. When he looked into the old man's eyes, Walks With Horse lifted his finger to his lips to quiet him. Will nodded his understanding as the old man removed his hand as he glanced over at the sleeping men lined around the dwindling fire.

Walks With Horse pulled out a knife and cut the ropes that bound Will's hands. When he was free, Will turned his arm over and saw that his right hand was pale and numb from the ropes binding him too tightly. He flexed his fingers to try to close his hand, but they were not cooperating very well. It would take some time before he could regain regular movement in his hand, if ever, but it was time they did not have. He would have to address it later and hope for the best.

Walks With Horse stood and motioned for Will to follow him. Will tried to place his feet out in front of him to start walking, but the fogginess in his brain was interfering. He struggled to take even a step, having difficulty balancing himself. He stood quietly and tried to focus all his remaining strength on moving his legs forward. He desperately needed some water, his thirst almost unquenchable.

The old man, who had started out in front, had turned back to see Will struggling, possibly about to fall, and walked back to help him. He could tell from the look in Will's eyes that he was in trouble.

He slung Will's arm around his neck as he put his arm around Will's waist and helped move him in the direction of the horses. Will fought to see out of his swollen eye at the campfire that Bell and his men were sleeping soundly around. He tried to remain quiet and stifle the pain that was radiating from his head down through his side, but it was taking all of his resolve not to call out from the hurt. He had to remain quiet. With not a gun between them, if someone awoke now, there would be no time for more questioning, and both he and the old man would be as good as dead.

They continued moving, slowly but continually, crouching as low as they could, not more than thirty feet from the men's fire. The old man was moving in a wide circle around the campsite, putting as much distance as he could between them and Bell's men. His movements were silent, almost invisible. Will was still somewhat disoriented and had to rely on the old man's help to make it through the darkness as he held his hand out in front of him to deflect anything that might be an obstacle.

After much effort, they finally made it over to the horses, but to Will's surprise, Walks With Horse did not stop there, but continued on past them. Will started to ask the reason why, but knew even the slightest bit of noise could awaken someone. He found out where they were heading before he could speak.

Walks With Horse had already moved two of the horses over by themselves for him and Will to ride. Will was glad to see that one of them was the buckskin.

As they passed the other horses, he was surprised as he caught a glimpse of the body of a man, who had obviously been on guard duty a short distance from the others, partially concealed by brush, lying back in the tall grass. *That was why he had not seen one on guard.* Will recognized him as being the one who had struck him with the rifle butt. His throat had been cut.

Finally, they made it to their horses. Walks With Horse leaned Will against the buckskin's saddle long enough to remove his arm from around his waist and help him lift his foot into the stirrup so he could climb into the saddle. It took all of his effort to swing his leg over his horse, and even more not to call out from the stabbing pain, but he finally made it while holding back the voicing of his discomfort. Even once he was in the saddle, he leaned forward, having difficulty keeping himself upright, the stabbing pain in his midsection and his distorted thinking all but getting the best of him. He struggled until he was finally able to sit up as he looked down at the old man, who gave Will the reins and then a solid nod. Will nodded back in quiet agreement.

For the first time, Will noticed that one of the men's gun belt and gun were hanging around the pommel and surmised that Walks With Horse had taken it off of the guard he had killed. He patted it for good luck.

Will tried to hold on to the reins with his right hand as he customarily did, but the blood had still not fully returned to it and he was having difficulty clenching his fist so he was left with no other option but to hold them in his left hand. He feared they would be forced into a shootout before they could get away, knowing his gun hand would be virtually useless to him.

He glanced over as Walks With Horse climbed into the saddle of one of Bell's men's horses and gave Will one final nod as Will tightened his grip on the reins in anticipation, just as the buckskin neighed gently.

Suddenly, they saw one of the men sleeping around the fire abruptly sit up from hearing the sound and look directly at them, speechless, his eyes wide with shock.

Walks With Horse let out a scream.

CHAPTER TEN

The blood-curdling scream of the old man sent everything instantly into panicked motion.

The campsite came to life with a blur of activity and chaos as everyone was startled from their sleep while they scrambled to try to figure out what was happening. Each man was searching for their guns while, at the same time, trying to get a grip on what had suddenly caused them to be violently awakened.

Will didn't hesitate and kicked the buckskin into motion just as he heard Bell and his men yelling in confusion. He had been so preoccupied with remaining quiet and staying in the saddle that he failed to notice that the old man had untied all of Bell's horses from their picket line. When the old man screamed, he followed it with two gunshots that sent all of their horses running towards the far end of the gulch at the same time that Will and the old man went running for the opposite end. By the time Bell and his men realized what was happening and had recovered their guns, Will's buckskin and the old man's horse were around the corner out of sight and running at a full gallop without any shots being fired by Bell and his men. They didn't stop until they had placed over two miles between them and the camp.

When Will finally pulled the buckskin to a stop, he looked behind him for signs that they were being followed, but quickly realized that they were safe. He glanced over at the old man and smiled. "Where'd you get the gun?"

"From man I killed."

"Well, thank you," he uttered as he fought to remain upright in the saddle, his body suddenly going limp. He felt himself slipping over to the side, unable to catch himself just as he felt a hand reach out and catch him by the shoulder and lean him upright in the saddle again.

He was disoriented as he saw the old man's hand reach over and take hold of the buckskin's reins and start leading him down the trail farther into the wilderness. He was trying to ask the old man where they were going when he passed out.

He lost track of time until he awakened again, some hours later lying next to a campfire under his blanket. Walks With Horse was tending to the fire and sampling a piece of fresh rabbit he had cooked. When he saw Will open his eyes, he pulled off a piece of meat and leaned over to hand it to him.

"You must eat to get back strength," the old man

said as he offered Will the meat. He took it and nodded to him out of gratitude.

"Thanks," he said, as he quickly devoured the first bite. It felt good to finally have some food in him, and it felt as if he could not chew fast enough to satisfy his stomach cravings. His lips were dry and parched, but that would have to wait until he had a little bit of food in him. The old man handed Will a canteen, which he grabbed and started drinking water as fast as he could swallow, his thirst overwhelming him. He got ahead of himself and choked on a mouthful, forcing him to pull it away so he could catch his breath. He laid down the canteen and resumed eating the rabbit as Walks With Horse pulled off his own portion and sat back to enjoy it while Will devoured two more bites before he paused long enough to speak.

"How long have I been out?" He was finally able to ask.

"Most of day," the old man responded as he stifled a cough and then took another bite. "Beating was bad," he added. "Tried to keep you alive. Think for some time maybe you die."

"I would have if it hadn't been for you," Will admitted freely before taking another quick bite. "Thank you."

"Bad men not follow us," the old man stated. "Watched for them over hill. No follow," he added as he pointed back from where they had traveled. "Still finding horses."

"How did you find me?" Will asked as he took a bite.

"Not hard. Bad men leave many tracks."

Will was surprised by the admission. "You followed me on foot?"

"Yes."

"Why did you follow me?"

"You help Walks With Horse. Me watch over you."

"So you saw them when they caught me."

He nodded. "Saw bad men beat you. Too many of them."

"Yeah," Will agreed. "You could have never taken all of them on. It was better for you to wait."

"Bad men drink heavy at night. Fall asleep. Easy to sneak into camp." The old man reached on the other side of him and picked up Will's gun, gun belt, and rifle. "This for you."

Will gladly reached over and took the weapons. "I thought I'd never see these again, or anything else for that matter. Thank you."

"You rest now," the old man suggested as he walked off to collect more wood. Will leaned back and savored another bite of the meat, thankful that the old man had come along when he had.

Will ate and drank his fill of water and then slept for several more hours, his body needing the rest from feeling battered and in pain. He felt a sense of relief that they hadn't been discovered. It was obvious that Bell and his men were not going to find them if they hadn't caught up with them by now. He was lucky to be alive, thanks to the old man.

He sat up in his bedding and glanced over at the old man, who was adjusting the harness on his horse's saddle. He had already saddled the buckskin, as well. Will glanced down at his right hand and flexed it to try to fend off the soreness and numbness. The color was finally back and as far as movement, it was almost back to normal, a welcome sight for him since it was highly likely that he would need his gun hand before this was over with.

He stood and had started gathered his bedding when the old man walked back over to the fire.

"You better. I go now," he said as he picked up his bedding. "You go to Kawnteenowah?"

"Yeah," Will answered softly, although not as proud to say it as he had been before. "I just want to see it for myself."

"White man find only bad medicine there, Travis," he responded in a final attempt to discourage him. Will could tell the old man was disappointed that he was still pursuing the notion, but despite whatever he thought, he didn't say anything else about it, probably because he knew it would do him no good. Will followed him over to the horses.

"Thanks again," Will said as they shook hands.

"Walks With Horse your friend. May the spirits watch over you, Travis," Walks With Horse said as he climbed into the saddle and waved one last time to

Will. As he rode away, Will wondered if he would ever see his friend again.

Will took another much-needed nap and ate some more before he decided it was time to put some more distance between him and Bell and his men. After breaking camp, Will rode west towards the outer edge of the gulch and straight towards Lakota territory. He had no clear idea exactly where Kawnteenowah was, so he was going to have to wander a bit in order to find it.

He paused as he stared at the base of the mountains ahead of him, looking back for movement or the sight of dust being stirred up by approaching riders. He could see for several miles, plenty of distance to give him a good head start even if he were being pursued, but there was nothing to see. He breathed a sigh of relief as he wheeled his horse around and back on his trail.

The Lakota territory was vast. Many did not realize just how much area it covered because they were too afraid of confronting the Lakota to find out. He could see the mountain ranges ahead of him and off to his sides growing in size, their massive presence being nothing short of intimidating. The sheer size meant he would have no way of knowing when he was truly on Lakota territory and when he wasn't, and no way to find out just short of running into some of the natives and by then, it would be too late to turn back.

He would have to take a different path through
the remainder of Hangman's Gulch to see if it took
him to Kawnteenowah. It was not the typical path to
Lakota land, but he needed to know if it could be
used as an alternate route for him or if he was going
to have to settle for taking his chances going straight
through Lakota territory. It wasn't his ideal situation
to ride into the country blindly, but it was the only
way he could do it.

It had been made clear to him that the path
through the mountains was not to taken lightly. It
was filled with steep embankments, cliffs, and other
obstacles that made the journey on horseback exceptionally difficult. There would also be the constant
concern of rocks becoming dislodged, especially from
the dramatic temperature changes the rocks would be
forced to endure, the constantly expanding and
contracting of the rock making it unstable, especially
for the footing of a horse.

He hesitated to choose the path through the
mountains, but as much as he hated to admit it, this
was still his best option. The Lakota would be less
likely to camp there, and if Bell and his men were
trailing him, at least they would think twice before
following him through such an arduous journey.

The route he was now using might not be suitable
for a herd of wild horses, but he still needed to be
sure that this wasn't a way to get them out of the
canyon. The terrain would be rough, but just how
rough he wasn't sure until he encountered it. If it

didn't work out, then running them through Lakota territory and then Hangman's Gulch would be his only other option, and one that he was not at all thrilled about being left with.

He traveled for some time without seeing anyone or anything, which he thought odd. This was a rugged country he was traveling into and he was wise to keep an eye out at all times.

The Lakota had adapted to living here for hundreds of years, but it was still considered brutal country for settlers and drifters to endure, especially on horseback. That kept many unwanted visitors off of Lakota land.

By the time it began to turn dark, he was ready to stop. His strength had not fully returned and his body was still recovering from the beating he had taken. What he needed now more than anything was to rest. But first, he had to find somewhere to take it.

He stopped at the outskirts of a grove of trees and quickly fashioned a lean-to in preparation for the cloudy weather he had been keeping an eye on all throughout the day. In no time, he had a fire going and was leaning back in his overturned saddle listening to the wind slide its way across the face of the mountains while he sipped piping hot coffee.

After eating, he stepped outside the lean-to and sipped his coffee while he took in his surroundings. Off in the distance, maybe a few hours away, maybe less, were some ominous-looking clouds, growing in strength, and they appeared to be heading straight in his direction. From the looks of them, he was glad to have already buckled down for the night.

Deep claps of thunder rumbled and announced its impending arrival. Flashes of distant lightning lit up the terrain, offering up sporadic glimpses of what to expect.

Will checked to make sure the buckskin was fine and of the approaching storm. He made it a point to keep watch over the buckskin, knowing the animal would alert him to things he would not pick up on himself. Horses had the ability to sense things that a human would easily overlook and out here, especially after what he had already gone through. He needed that keen sense of perception more than ever.

Satisfied the buckskin was alright, he gathered another generous armful of firewood and went back inside the lean-to and prepared for the storm that was coming. He had fed the fire some more and laid back, finishing off his coffee, when he began to notice something odd. There were no noises of the nighttime.

In fact, it was quiet.

An eerie quiet.

There was virtually no breeze and none of the usual sounds of the wilderness that he expected to hear were there. It was as if the whole countryside had shut down in anticipation of something coming that was massive, powerful, and beyond their control. Even the coyote that had serenaded him while he scouted a campsite and built his lean-to had since become silent. But the buckskin had not alerted to anything, so he dismissed it as being nothing, which could mean only one thing: a storm was coming in the not-too-distant future.

There was no more preparation to be made. This was where he would be forced to ride out the oncoming weather. He only hoped that the precautions he had taken would somehow be enough.

Will stuck his head out from under the confines of the lean-to and took notice of the sky. Now that the last hints of daylight had slid behind the mountain range, the sky was darkening, but tonight it was doing so more than usual. This was not a typical nighttime sky. When he glanced up, all he could see was total blackness and there were no stars to be found anywhere. The air was noticeably thicker, with a weighted dampness that was customary to occur before a storm. Will braced for the worst as far as storms went.

This was going to be a bad one.

CHAPTER ELEVEN

It was midmorning by the time Bell watched three of his men ride into their camp on their horses. He wondered why there were still three men missing.

Bell's jaw tightened from his suppressed anger. He had been sitting there alone, next to the fire, for the remainder of the night and half of the morning since the drifter's escape. Thinking. Plotting. Stewing in his own anger. He had misjudged the drifter, if that was, in fact, what he really was, and his misjudgment had cost him.

Cost him dearly.

He should have killed him outright, right then and there, as soon as he had spotted him. He knew that now, though it was after the fact. That's what he had always done whenever a stranger wandered into their hideout. But this time, for some unknown reason, he had decided to question the man for information. Now look what had happened. Not only did he not get any answers, but he had lost a man in the process.

He took a sip of coffee, which was too hot, and burned his mouth before he realized that he had just made the pot. He cursed himself for being such a fool, with the coffee and with his dealings with the drifter. He was trying to calm down, but he was furious with himself. Now he was so distracted by the turn of events that he had now scalded his mouth on top of everything else. He threw the cup down in anger and turned to face his men as one of them separated from the other two and walked closer.

"'Bout time you made it back," he jabbed at them with discontent. "What took you so long?"

"We couldn't very well find 'em in the dark, Bell," one of the men, Jed Castle, said. "We walked around the rest of the night looking for 'em, but you can't track horses at night."

Bell looked past the man at the two behind him, as if he were looking for someone that wasn't there. "Where's Arturo, Renslow and Jacobs?"

"Still tracking their horses," Castle offered as he tied his off on the picket line.

"Then why aren't you helping them?" Bell asked, his voice filled with irritation, picking out the man's mistakes.

"Let 'em find their own horses," Castle argued. "We had to find ours." Castle walked over closer to the fire, picked up one of the coffee cups sitting on a large rock and was reaching for the coffeepot when

Bell hit him. Castle was not expecting the hit and fell backwards onto the ground with a grunt. He lifted his head, shaking it to try to clear the cobwebs that distorted his thinking. "What'd you do that for?!" He yelled as he rubbed his damaged jaw.

"You were supposed to bring back the horses," Bell shouted back with an accusatory finger pointed at Castle. "*All* the horses!"

"It was bad enough just trying to find ours," Jed Castle stated profoundly as he slowly got to his feet, still favoring his jaw. "Why do I have to help them find theirs, too?"

"Because we need those horses, *that's* why!" Bell shouted as he turned back to the fire while trying to slow his breathing. "It's bad enough we let that drifter go."

"We didn't let him go! He escaped! We left chasing the horses so quick I didn't get to find out what all happened," Castle said.

Bell exhaled sharply as he spoke. "Someone cut him loose. An Indian. The one you saw riding off with him."

"How could he come into camp and cut that fella loose and not be heard?"

"It had to be him because the drifter didn't have a knife and the ropes were cut. It was him alright."

Castle glanced all around the camp as a thought suddenly occurred to him. "Where's Warner?"

"He's dead."

"*Dead?*" Castle quickly turned back to Bell as he

questioned the statement in disbelief. "What happened to him?"

"His throat was cut."

"The Indian!"

"Yeah. The Indian. They took his gun, too, And a horse."

"What are we gonna do now?"

Bell stared into the fire, not wanting to admit what he was about to say. "We'll have to let him go, at least for now."

"*What?*" Castle exclaimed. "Why are we going to let him go?"

"Because not everyone is back and we don't have all of our horses. We can't very well go after him riding double. Since we don't know which direction everybody went, we'll have to wait here until the others get back."

"Can't we go looking for them?"

Bell cut the man a glare. "Do *you* know where they went?"

"Uh... no."

"Neither do I. And I don't want the rest of you to be wandering around the woods looking for one another, either. So we don't have a choice. We have to wait here until they get back."

Then are we going after him?"

"We'll check outside of here, but I don't want to go out too far."

Castle was reluctant to ask, but he finally found the courage to. "What about the drifter?"

Bell looked at him with cold, hard eyes. "I'll run into him again. And next time, when I do, I won't waste any time killing him."

After repositioning the saddle closer to the back of the lean-to, Will checked the buckskin's reins to make sure they were thoroughly secured to the tree they had taken shelter under. The weather was about to turn nasty and the last thing he needed was to be forced to track down a runaway horse in violent weather through the mountains. It would also be dangerous for the buckskin to be running around freely on the side of the mountain in the storm.

Judging from how blackened the sky had become, he thought it best to dig a moat around the lean-to to divert water away from it. There was ample firewood to at least last him through the night and even into early tomorrow, should a storm persist for that long.

The temperature continued to drop the closer the storm moved. He had ample wood to last him, but he feared the storm would last longer than anticipated and his supply would run out. He had done all he could do to prepare.

The night was wild and black as waves of thunder rumbled closer in the distance. The wind was suddenly colder from the approaching storm and the temperature dipped enough to force him to retrieve his coat.

An occasional flash of lightning lit up the entire

sky, giving off an eerie glow to the land at the wrong time of night, when there should not have been any. One such flash exposed the wall of gray rainwater skimming the surface a few miles out and heading his way. He braced for its impact. The wind that was carrying the storm to him was picking up and stirred the tree limbs wildly about as if it were trying to tear them from their place. The increased winds also brought with it tiny specks of sand that had been lifted from the ground and stung his face as they were thrown at him in swirling waves of a heavy breeze.

Leaves and other debris began to litter the land-scape, flowing sideways over the terrain, some even finding its way into his shelter as if being slid across the surface by a large invisible hand. The flap to his lean-to began to flutter in the building winds, giving him just enough time to properly secure it before the rain hit.

He was set for food with a pheasant that he had shot and cleaned earlier that had almost finished cooking. The only concern that he had now was from rocks being dislodged by the torrential rains and crashing down on top of him or the buckskin. If that happened, there would be no warning and nothing he could do about in the midsts of a savage storm.

He had chosen to pitch his shelter on the lower side of a pair of large Ponderosa pines, the largest ones anywhere around him, hoping that their deep-rooted systems would keep them in place and help deflect anything that came barreling down the side of

the mountain at them, especially at night in the dark.
The massive trees had obviously endured such storms
in the past and had survived. He felt it was a solid
decision to use them. As the night passed all around
him, he succumbed to the notion that it was all he
could do to protect the two of them.

The buckskin was noticeably distraught over the
coming storm, but there was nothing more that he
could do for it, and his only thought was to hope for
the best.

But now, the more he thought about the harsh
storm he was about to be in, the more he was having
second thoughts about their safety. Attempting to
move his camp at this late time would prove disastrous. There was no time, anyway. It was only a short
time later that he realized he had made the right
decision to stay put when he heard the first drops of
rain begin to fall.

As the rain pelted the top of the shelter, he kept
vigilance of the rubble that the cascading rain was
removing from the face of the mountain as he heard
it tumbling past him on both sides, but it had been
nothing close enough to matter and nothing of significant size. If the rocks being brought down it began
to increase in size, he would want to move his camp
and quickly, but to where he had no clue. Besides,
there would be no time to do so once the material of
the run-off turned to rocks. He would need to
stay put.

The torrential downpour continued for most of

the night, turning the side of the mountain into a soggy, slippery mess. Distorted bolts of lightning strangely illuminated the sky in short bursts, sending crackling cascades of fractured light across the sky in bizarre patterns followed by bellows of booming thunder. The wind howled with a blatant intensity, whipping the brush of the landscape without mercy and more than once threatening to destroy his shelter.

Gusts of wind were sending waves of stinging rain down on the countryside, sometimes so fierce that the winds caused them to blow almost sideways and pass over him. He secured the make-shift door as best he could, hoping the wind didn't become violent enough to rip it away and leaving him more vulnerable and exposed. The blackened night erupted with booming thunder that rumbled down to the core of the mountain, sometimes so close that it shook the ground underneath him. Twice he heard the buckskin neigh nervously, forcing him to glance outside at the horse's condition, but to the horse's credit, it made no other sounds to imply that it was in distress.

Multiple times, his shelter was threatened throughout the storm, his faith in its stability beginning to wane while the storm continued to pound down on him relentlessly hour after hour.

The buckskin had his own plight with the weather to contend with, signaling his concern at the storm's intensity and stepping nervously as the storm barreled down on them. Will had managed to tie the horse off where he could see Will, hoping that seeing his presence would help to keep the animal somewhat calm until the storm had passed.

More than once, the intensity and fierceness of the storm threatened his and the buckskin's existence on the side of the mountain. As the night seemed to drag on endlessly, the lean-to shifted several times under sudden bursts of extreme wind, but so far had managed to hold up to the storm's ferocity. Will periodically stuck his head outside to make sure the buckskin was still bearing the storm and to console him as best he could with his words, which offered the animal some relief, but he knew it was not enough for what it was having to endure.

Around midnight, the storm began to lessen for a brief time, giving Will hope that it was coming to an end. But the relief was short-lived as the next phase of the storm came at him with a vengeance, possibly even worse than the first part.

He continued feeding the fire to stay warm as shards of cooling, moist air found its way into the lean-to and stabbed at him. He bundled his coat closer around his neck to ward off its advances. The howling of the winds continually remained him of just how extreme the weather had become. Just as he began to relax, another bout of wind would smash into the side of his shelter and reignite his concern.

He would not get much sleep tonight.

CHAPTER TWELVE

Time was reduced to a crawl as the rain and the hammering winds of the storm seemed to drag on forever through the night, making it seem like it was lingering exponentially longer than it actually was. Will continued to worry about his shelter's integrity, but pushed the concern to the back of his mind since it was too late to do anything about it now. It was what he had made of it, for better or worse.

Waves of harsh winds slapped at and threatened him and the buckskin as he waited in uneasy fashion for the next gale to finish off his shelter and send him and his belongings tumbling down the slick mountainside to their end. For several more hours, he endured the wrath of the storm, each outburst of violent weather seeming to be as intense as the previous one and each one worrying him just as much.

Just when he thought he had endured the worst of

it, the brunt of the storm came sometime in the wee hours of the morning, bringing with it the harshest of conditions. And then it happened.

An hour before sunrise, he heard the massive, sickening cracking of wood as the top portion of one of the Ponderosa pines he had based the location of his lean-to on could not withstand the voracity of the storm any longer and snapped as it came plummeting down towards him. He felt helpless as he heard the sickening squeak of the wood's integrity giving way like a small green branch being snapped over a knee, as it twisted unnaturally and lost its battle with the wind. He had only a fleeting moment of warning to hope for the best that it would not land on top of him or the buckskin. A second later came the deafening crash of it landing just yards from his shelter. He heard the buckskin's displeasure through its frightened cries as the massive chunk of wood came to rest precariously close to them both.

It had been a long, dreary night of violent weather, but by daylight, the heavy rain had been reduced to nothing more than a sprinkle. As he stepped outside of the lean-to, he got a glimpse of just how close the tree had come to killing them both. They had been lucky.

The combination of his body's residual aching from the beating he had taken plus getting very little sleep during the storm made him slow getting up, hoping that the sky would clear enough soon so he could be on his way. By the time the weather did manage to break, he was saddled and gladly leaving his camp, eager to be back in the saddle as he headed farther up the mountain.

The buckskin was drenched to the bones and as eager to get moving as him. No doubt enduring a night of horrific weather, it had not been pleasant for the horse either, so leaving this area behind them as quickly as possible would be welcomed by them both.

The walls of the canyon were steep, almost too steep even to climb, which he had been forced into at some points. Still, their gradual ascent meant that it was much more of a risk of losing his horse to it. He would have to continue on the way he was heading with the hope that things would eventually ease up, but he wasn't convinced and had his doubts.

The sheer rock walls were stunning, spiraling upwards of a thousand feet into the sky. He had to get around them since climbing them on horseback was out of the question. Even if he managed to find a path or trail to follow, it would only allow for a man to pass and would certainly not be wide enough for the girth of a horse to safely pass through. He had convinced himself that there had to be a way around them that he hadn't yet come across, but even that belief was quickly fading away.

He carefully nudged the buckskin on, while trying not to push the animal too hard and stress him. He could tell the buckskin was choosing his steps carefully, for that he did not fault the animal. With slippery dislodged sheets of slate underfoot and the saturation of the ground from the storm, the buckskin had to be leery.

The horse was built for such demands, but even it was distrustful of the terrain. He could not blame him for his trepidation. At times, there was nothing but air on his left that fell away far enough that something as simple as a stumble would result in an injury that neither of them would be able to recover from, or worse. It would take very little pieces of rock careening down the slope on top of them to send him and his horse screaming down into the darkened abyss that lay below them. Even if they weren't sent to their deaths below, being injured out here would surely result in a slow, agonizing death from exposure or wild animals. For those reasons alone, it was not a place he preferred to dwell in any longer than was absolutely necessary. As treacherous as the going was, he had to keep moving.

He had misjudged the route coming across the mountains, that much was for certain to him now, but it was too little information, too late. He had anticipated the mountains opening up and exposing valleys and terrain that he could use this trip, but that had not happened. There was no turning back now. He understood that, although the realization was of little comfort to him in his present situation.

Will was lost in thought when he felt the buckskin's footing slip. The horse instantly panicked, trying to catch itself, but could not get a firm footing in the loose rock. Will needed to jump down to give the animal less to have to balance, but there was no time for that now. He struggled to stay in the saddle as the buckskin's body twisted to try to lean into the mountain and take the weight off of its front legs, which were having difficulty staying implanted against the rock. The buckskin scrambled for its footing, slipped, and scrambled again. It was slowly sliding down the hill, but had still somehow managed to maintain its footing.

Will loosened his grasp on the reins to give the buckskin all the slack he needed to turn his head to see the severity of its predicament. After what seemed like an eternity, the buckskin gathered his confidence and leveled out as he once again regained his footing. He snorted loudly to express his stress and his relief. The encounter helped Will decide it was time for him to go awhile on foot.

The land he traveled through was empty and desolate and had very little to offer that was appealing. Scrub oaks and foxtail pine dotted the mountainside with an occasional errant shrub and sagebrush bordering the trail, which wasn't that much of a trail to begin with, and offered very little as far as signs that animals had recently traversed it, especially since the rain the night before.

The air was fresh with the wind off the mountains, bringing with it the smell of fir trees as it cascaded down the trail past him. The only good thing about being here was that there would be no worry of water in these parts since pockets of it would be fed either from mountain streams or standing pools that had accumulated since it had rained.

He paused early on and stepped out onto a plateau to survey his surroundings and check his back trail while the buckskin grazed on the sparse patches of lush, untouched grasses around him. There was no one in sight for as far back as he could see. He had been away from Bell and his men long enough that even they were no longer a concern to him. Even if they had tried to follow him, their experience with the slopes and rough terrain would have been enough to convince them that Will wasn't worth it. Though he had no reason to believe otherwise, if anyone was following him, they were doing an excellent job of hiding their movements.

He wasn't exactly sure where he was, but he knew that by now he had to already be in Lakota territory. Besides the Lakota, Will also had to be on the lookout for Crow and Blackfoot, both of who had also settled in the area and co-existed there. Each of them preferred to be left alone and would not welcome seeing him there, so he had to constantly be on the lookout in case he needed to escape, especially since they would know the area far better than he did.

Will followed the trail for several more miles before he branched off to a side trail that looked to have an adequate amount of fresh tracks. There was no need to continue climbing up the mountain when there would be places along this trail that would provide substantial water. Besides, it stood to reason that if there were horses, they would most likely be in the lower part of the mountains.

He was running into piles of rock that had become dislodged and broken off from the canyon walls and had settled on the trail, forcing the animals that relied on it to divert their tracks around them. With the instability of the rock walls, it was just one more thing he had to be watching out for. Rocks of all sizes were at risk of falling at any time and without warning, with some being almost as large as the buckskin. If he were caught here by a landslide, there would be nowhere to run and even less chance of getting out alive.

All morning, Will couldn't shake the notion of how precarious his position was on the side of the mountain. The occasional banging of a falling rock and the echo that it created as it bounced and tumbled down the face of the mountain into nothingness reinforced how dangerous a rockslide would be for him. He then realized thinking about it also gave him pause for another reason. What if the entrance to the valley of the horses was blocked with fallen rocks? That would certainly explain why the horses had never left the valley. If that were the case, there would be no way for him to dig it out and not only would his being there make no difference in freeing them, but he would have put his life, and that of the buckskin, in jeopardy for nothing, making his presence there on Lakota land even harder to explain.

He spent the remainder of the day moving and weaving through the rocks as he continued across the side of the mountain. It was slow going and he could tell the strain of climbing and trying to maintain his footing on the unsteady land was taking its toll on the buckskin. He rode when the trail permitted and twice, when the rock below the buckskin's feet became too treacherous, he dismounted to ease the animal's burden. He felt bad that he had subjected the buckskin to such precarious travel, but it was the only way for him to verify if it was going to be a viable escape route for the horses. Now that he had established it wasn't, they needed to get out of there and off the mountain as quickly and as safely as possible.

It was beginning to get dark when he decided to bed down for the night, his mental state as exhausted as his body. The buckskin appeared as relieved to call it a day as he was.

He had happened upon a small pool that had collected from the recent rains, which seemed as good of a place as any he would likely find. He stripped the saddle from the buckskin and let him drink his fill. While the horse grazed on the grass, Will took his drink and then refilled the canteen, just in case it was required of him to leave in a hurry.

Spent from the demands of the day, he walked across the wall face and found an indentation that set back into the steep wall a good ten feet or more. Normally, he would not consider having a fire on the side of a mountain for fear that it would give him away, but with the rock cut out here and the high wall to his right, he felt safe enough with one. Besides, if he didn't have a fire, it would be a long, cold night.

He wasn't too concerned with being spotted, anyway. If he couldn't see down into the valley he had just crossed, then a rider would likely not be able to see his fire from their vantage point down below.

After gathering some kindling, he had a fire going with a pot of coffee brewing while he ate from his stash of jerky and biscuits.

After eating, he sat back in his saddle and sipped his coffee while he looked across the landscape. The canyon was quiet, almost too quiet for him and leaving him feeling a little too exposed. There was a faint, continuous breeze that channeled past him, that was slowly cooling off with the approaching night. The walls of the mountain echoed the scarce sounds of the night that he would expect from being on the side of a mountain. In the distance, he heard a coyote call out to another that failed to respond. The sound brought the buckskin's head to rise briefly, but then lowered it to continue grazing when he felt they were not a threat.

As he sat by the fire and relaxed, he tried to work some of the tension and soreness from his joints. He still had not fully recovered from the beating he had endured, the pain from his injured side making itself known much too often for his liking and the swelling of his one eye still somewhat lingering. At least his gun hand had recovered, but the rest of his body needed more time. He eased back into his saddle and tilted his hat over his eyes, trying to relax and catch up on his lost night of sleep. With his movements being stiffened and slower than usual, he felt vulnerable and out here, being vulnerable was a good way to end up dead.

CHAPTER THIRTEEN

Sometime after midnight, he was startled awake by the sound of a falling stone bouncing off points of the wall until it made it somewhere below at the bottom of the canyon, his body tensing, not realizing that he had dozed off at some point. The abrupt awakening took him off guard for a split second until he gathered his thoughts to remind himself where he was.

With his gun drawn, he stood and took a few steps closer to the indented opening of the rocks. He stood silent, listening for anything. It was true that falling rocks were a normal occurrence in these mountains, but it was also something that he couldn't take for granted. Typically, something would have caused the rock to fall. Was it due to a change in temperature causing the rocks to constrict and expand, or was it dislodged by something, or someone? He had to make sure.

He waited and listened, but heard nothing more.

Was he making more out of this than there should be? Perhaps, but out here, he didn't have the luxury of taking things for granted. The nighttime could play tricks on a man's mind and fool his senses into thinking that there were other things out there patrolling the night that he couldn't see. If it was someone trying to sneak up on him, they would have caused more than one rock to fall, considering how treacherous scaling these walls in the dark would be. If it were an animal, it would likely be a mountain lion prowling the cool of the night looking for a meal, which caused him to worry for the buckskin.

For his own peace of mind, he moved his bedding on the front side of the fire, where he could keep a better eye on his horse. Once again, he would not be getting much sleep for the rest of the night, that was for sure.

He listened intently for a while, but no other sounds were made out there in the dark. Once he finally felt assured that it was just a random, harmless incident, he closed his eyes with his rifle by his side and his Colt lying on the top of his blanket.

The rest of the night came and went without incident. As morning showed itself, he rose and quickly ate and was on his way before the sun barely had enough time to fully show. The bite of the cooler air helped stir his senses and got him moving. As he pulled the buckskin into service, he decided he would continue following the side trail he had been taking in the hopes that it would level out soon, and he could find an easier way across the remainder of the mountain.

Much to his relief, after traveling for most of the morning, the trail began to become easier, and he started making better time. He continued to periodically check his back trail, but there were still no signs that he was being followed.

At just after midday, he came upon a plateau. He had finally reached the top edge of the mountain he had been skirting for almost three days. He could see why there were few tracks this way other than scattered remnants of wild game. He also found out that he could not bring a herd of horses the way he had come. With such a treacherous climb, it would be impossible to contain them, let alone lead them.

The route he had come on had taken considerably longer than he had anticipated. He did not have the time to add to his journey. At least now he knew that he would have to find a different trip back. That meant staying on Lakota land longer and having to go around Hangman's Gulch. That would add more days to his trip, something he did not relish, but it was something that could not be helped.

Soon after he topped the mountain, the trail began to descend at a gradual pace. The surroundings were strewn with sagebrush and twisted spurs of pine while hazardous loose rock that had been shaken loose by the torrential rains littered the path. Even though it looked passable, he would have to be careful. One misstep from the buckskin and the animal would easily be crippled and being alone out here in Lakota territory without a horse it would be a toss up as to which got to him first, the Lakota or a wild animal.

He stopped at the first watering hole he came to and gave the buckskin a breather while they both drank deeply to their content. Will cupped handfuls of the cold mountain runoff and splashed his face and the back of his neck for relief, the trails of runoff sliding down the front of his neck and onto his chest, its icy fingers gliding across his sweaty skin. He cupped another handful and tossed it onto the back of his head, where he had been bleeding from being struck with the rifle butt. The shock of the water's coldness helped to relieve some of the nagging discomfort from wearing his hat and worked to temporarily numb the injured area, at least for a little while.

Leaning back against a large boulder, he tilted his hat back to relieve some of the sweat that had built on his forehead as he studied the terrain in front of him. From here, he had an unobstructed view for many miles in front of him. With so many places for a valley to be situated and not being sure which direction he must travel, he had his work cut out for him. We took another deep drink from his canteen and exhaled its satisfaction.

When they had rested a spell, he topped off the canteen once again and decided to walk the buckskin for a while to give him a rest. The animal had been worked hard these last three days, being driven through much uneven ground with plenty of loose rocks and the remnants of a past storm, and deserved to be riderless for a change. Besides, the loose rock underfoot was still worrying Will that the buckskin could take a bad step and break his leg. He stood a better chance if he did not have to worry about the weight of a rider on his back.

He continued scaling the mountain face, hugging the rock wall as much as possible. The going was slow, necessarily slow considering the terrain, but in time he was able to maneuver his way down a considerable distance and before long, the landscape was starting to level out more and they found themselves getting closer to the bottom.

A wave of relief passed over him as the tree line finally came up to meet them. Will was happy to be off the mountain at last and back where he could make up some of the time he had not anticipated losing. But being back down also meant that it was more likely for him to run into others, namely the Lakota.

He had thought about what he would say was his reasoning for being on their land, his reasoning for looking for something he had no right to take, but nothing legitimate enough came to mind. For now, he would have to play it by ear and hope he wasn't spotted.

After a good hour in the saddle, Will happened upon the entrance of an abandoned mine nestled in the crook of the mountain's base. It was all grown over with shrubs and weeds, proving that it had not been worked in quite some time. The timbers to the entrance were rotted and sitting at a precarious angle from starting to cave in and the small pile of discorded mining tools were rusted and covered liberally with earth and other sediment, courtesy of being exposed to the elements for what looked like years. A cloud of dust slowly permeated from the mine's opening, giving off a stagnant, putrid odor of the mine's long ago deserted contents. Right outside the entrance, a small mining cart had been tipped over onto its side by a haphazard boulder that had, at some point, become dislodged from above and crashed into it, caving in one whole side of the cart.

He had spotted what could have been small mining areas along the creeks and streams he had encountered where it looked like the landscape had been altered somewhat by pick and shovel, but it was hard to discern for certain. Panning for gold was always a guessing game and usually required uprooting and moving the operation along various points of a body of moving water as a location refused to offer up anything of value.

There were stories of there being gold in these mountains, he had heard some of them himself, stories that had been passed around for some years, but prospectors were not inclined to look for it for fear of running into the Lakota or some other tribes. No substantial amount of gold had ever been declared as having come from these mountains, but that didn't dissuade those who were struck with the fever to try their hand at finding it.

No one knew if their failure at finding something was due to the gold not being there or if they had fallen victim as trespassers before they were able to recover it. Either way, the notion of mining for it was outweighed by the more realistic threat of being killed by the Lakota.

With fall approaching, it was cooling off more at night and over the majority of the day, which meant there was less heat in the day, leaving spots that were still damp from the torrential downpour a couple of days earlier. He would use this to his advantage since it made traveling easier as the saturated ground produced less noise than moving over dried and brittle foliage and the granite walls allowed sound to carry for a considerable distance.

Out here alone, with no knowledge of the area and little to no possibility of finding refuge from being caught out in the open, from this point on, it was important for them to make as little noise as possible. No doubt they were already in Lakota land and, as such, he needed every advantage he could get and not to announce his presence there.

Since finding out that the route he had taken to get there was not going to allow horses to be run back through it, he worried about how he was going to move the horses to bring them back. It was not unlikely that he could bring them across Lakota land

and through Hangman's Gulch, but the more he could steer clear of those areas, the better off he would be.

Once the Lakota discovered what he was doing, and he feared it wouldn't take them long to do so, they would not be at all tolerant of his actions. But if by some miracle he managed to release the horses before he was discovered, it would be a race to see how quickly he could get them out of the territory before the Lakota caught on to him. And once he had them moving, there would be no stopping them. Stopping them meant getting caught. Stopping them meant being branded a thief. Stopping them meant a slow and painful death.

He rode for a while longer as the day eased on. His sole intent now was to look for anything that could resemble the rim of a canyon, probably one that was off the beaten path. The more veiled, the better. There would likely be no path or trail to give away its location and it was certain to be well-hidden. Finding it would not be easy, and the longer he was made to wander around the area, the more likely it was that he would run into the Lakota.

Will sensed that his horse was becoming spent when he began to look for a place to set up camp for the night. Wherever he chose, it needed to be back in the trees, since the dense canopy would be necessary to break up the smoke generated from a fire, if he dared make one. He would need as many advantages to disguise his presence here as possible.

When he rounded a group of trees was when he saw it. In the mud, right there in front of him, in plain sight. It was what he had hoped not to see this quickly.

Footprints.

CHAPTER FOURTEEN

Will instantly pulled back on the buckskin's reins, carefully surveying the land around him and listening intently as he slowly drew his Colt. He turned the buckskin around to see behind him and then back to the footprints. An uneasy feeling crept over him.

The sight of the footprints worried him, and for good reason. He had no idea how close he was to the canyon, if he was even close at all. Without sufficient landmarks to go by, he could be relatively close to it and never realize it, causing him to wander aimlessly for who knew how long until he was forced to give up his search or become discovered and flee for his life. But, then again, he had to ease his need. It was dangerous to be here, but he had traveled this far. He couldn't go back now. Not empty-handed.

Going back meant he would never get another chance to look for it. He would never make it through Hangman's Gulch again, and he certainly wouldn't consider putting the buckskin's life on the line going through the mountains around it. It had been more than just dumb luck that had brought them this far. It been a miracle that he had made it through the first time. He had already come so far that the thought of having to abandon his search at this late date was a notion he didn't care to entertain. He had nothing to lose.

His eyes continued to carefully take in his surroundings as the only sound made was the cocking of the Colt's hammer. He heightened his hearing as best he could. If there were Lakota around, they would be hard to detect, almost silent in their movements. But hopefully the best that he could hope for was that he could pick up the sound of a horse moving about.

The sight of the footprints was also unnerving to him because of how recently they would have to have been made. It had been two-and-a-half days since the last rain. For them to have remained visible, these prints would had to have been made since then. But how often did they come through here? Was it a routine hunting area for them? Did that mean that their village was close by? Or the valley?

Will paused in the saddle, waiting and listening, his eyes as much on the lookout as his ears. He glanced down at the buckskin to judge for his reaction, but the animal didn't signal that anything, or anyone, was out there. The lack of a reaction from the buckskin was somewhat comforting. He had grown to trust the horse's instincts, which had saved his hide more than once.

He adjusted in his saddle, almost cringing at the creaking sound that doing so generated. It took several minutes for him to reassure himself that the individuals who had made the tracks had been gone for some time. If any of them were still in the area, they would have descended on him by now.

Finally convinced there was nothing of an immediate threat, he uncocked and holstered his gun and climbed down to closer inspect the tracks, taking one final glance at his surroundings before he knelt down to satisfy his instincts. The tracks were smooth with no manufactured heel.

Moccasins.

As he stood, he took still another glance around him, not really sure whether to second guess if he trusted his instincts that he was alone out here. He convinced himself that everything was fine and climbed into his mount, not wanting to be caught on the ground if an attack was to happen. His hesitance lessened, but not completely dismissed. One thing was for certain: he was now definitely on Lakota land.

Lakota had a reputation for not wandering past their own reservation. They were an overall peaceful tribe and did not wage a fight unless one was brought to them. Will knew the Lakota would not be accepting of his presence there, especially when he could not divulge why he was there. To them, it would be a simple case of trespassing that they would not take lightly. But knowing the real reason for his presence, there would be detrimental to his health since no one voluntarily wandered onto the Lakota reservation. If they ever found out why he was there, he would be a dead man for sure.

After checking around the prints further, he discovered that there were several sets of tracks spread a small distance apart, so whoever they were, they were staying close to one another. He had no idea how many natives had come through there, but judging from the tracks, there appeared to be at least three of them. Luckily, they were long gone. But what reason would they have had for being there? *Hunting party perhaps? Or maybe scouts? But why would they need to scout their own land unless they suspected someone was there that shouldn't be? Someone like him?*

Will kept his eyes open as he started moving again, not liking that he was feeling as if he were being hunted. Whether that was the case didn't matter to him. He still felt uneasy. But, like to or not, it was a feeling he didn't see losing anytime soon.

He kept a watch over the horse's reactions, still relying on him to give him fair warning of someone approaching. Being tense about the situation he was now in annoyed him. He saw no one, although it didn't feel that way as far as reassuring him that he was alone. Besides, if he were dealing with the

Lakota, chances are he wouldn't see them until they were already on him.

He was seriously questioning if coming here had been a mistake, one that would surely cost him his life.

Will Travis spent the remainder of the day following faint game trails that wound down through the rocky crevasses and pointed him towards the canyon floor. The trail down was narrow and treacherous, to say the least, and its cramped quarters and limited visibility slowed his travel. He noticed that the trail ahead of him had grown darker, but he didn't know why. It was almost dusk when he realized why when he happened upon the edge of some lava beds.

Although he could not see the extent of the beds, he had to assume that the blackened layer spread for a considerable distance on the surface and probably much farther underneath. With the consistency of lava, it was impossible to determine how long ago these passages and paths had been formed since, unlike dirt, they did not weather away or erode from the rains. It was also impossible to determine how old they were. Were these beds formed recently enough to trap horses or had they been there for centuries?

The lava covered everything in its path and rendered it all to look the same. Tunnels were often created when the lava hardened on the surface while the molten flow continued underneath, carving a path for it through solid rock as if running a hot knife through softened butter. As the lava flow cut away at the sedentary rock, it cooled and left behind a hollowed network of tunnels of varying sizes, which remained largely unseen from above and could easily stretch for miles. It also made for treacherous traveling. A horse's hoof could easily slip into a hole in the lava and snap, leaving the animal crippled.

The lava beds were of considerable interest to him because of how they were formed. Despite being hot enough to scorch anything in its path, lava, like water, would seek the path of last resistance so there would be places where the lava flowed around an obstruction of some kind such as a massive collection of rocks jetting out from the earth, as in the walls of a canyon. Diverting the path of the lava would leave the ground inside these diversions to thrive. This would create small islands of grazeable land where the grass was untouched and fed by the high mineral content left behind by the lava. With abundant water from the mountain runoffs, such a place could easily sustain animal life.

Animal life, such as horses.

It had never occurred to him before, but the formation of the lava beds made perfect sense for supporting horses. He realized the sight of the hardened lava was the perfect cover. Those seeing it for the first time would not expect it to leave anything in its wake, especially grasses. With the enormous covering of blackened lava being laid out in front of them as far as the eye could see, it would likely not occur to someone traveling through that there could be exposed land beyond it that had been left untouched by the scorching heat.

The sight of the lava beds would cause a person to believe that nothing could live in such a harsh environment. Unless that person continued further into the beds to investigate, they were unlikely to see any land that had become trapped during it being formed. That was enough of a reason for him to continue.

He followed the faint trail around as he slowly descended into the lower country. The hardened lava had not only carved a path into the rock, but the formation of new rock shelves had helped to divert any runoff of water from the mountains. The water would not be allowed to flow in the hollowed recesses of the lava flowing underneath the surface and would instead end up in any naturally formed valley that might have been unintentionally created. If this water had been allowed to accumulate or even flow through such a valley, it would provide everything that was needed to sustain life. And with no one to disturb them, wild horses would be left alone to breed and thrive with everything they needed at their disposal and no natural predators to be fearful of, including man.

Will skirted the rim of the lava beds looking for a way in, but after some time, he was having no luck in doing so. He climbed from his saddle and led the buckskin. He studied the area, looking for some sort of trail that could lead him in, but with the hardened consistency of the lava, it was brutally impossible to find tracks of any kind from either man or animal.

The afternoon was withering away as he scaled the rim of the canyon, looking for a way in. The brush was scattered here, and there was no sign of water in the immediate area, but that did not dissuade his search. There was something there. Just beyond his sight. He could feel it.

He came upon a drop-off of enough height that the buckskin would not be able to maneuver through it safely, forcing him to divert his path around it. *There had to be a trail of some kind around there*. It was just a matter of finding where it originated. The same thing happened again, but while it was discouraging, it did not make him want to quit his search. He just had to keep looking until he could find the path that other animals had taken to find nearby water.

He came upon a wall of hardened lava that had created a cutoff for the trail, but he knew there had to be a way around it. He had picked up on some scratch marks on the lava that appeared to be from larger hooded animals, like deer or elk, that had also wandered here, at some point, looking for water. They were the only animals he could rely on that were large and heavy enough to have left tracks on the hardened lava. But with no water in sight, it meant there had to be water close by. His concern was well deserved. He had not run out of water as yet, but it was starting to concern him that he was having a difficult time finding it. If this wasn't a way to it, there had to be another path he hadn't come across, as of yet.

He had to keep looking. If other animals had found it, so could he.

CHAPTER FIFTEEN

Will pressed on, losing daylight quicker than he wanted and finding nothing in the process. The stuff marks on the lava were undeniable. All he had to do was follow them and eventually, they had to lead him to water. But he couldn't very well travel through here after dark and he needed water.

He stopped at a small cropping of long grass that had exposed itself to the sun through a diversion of the lava flow. The area was small, but would give the buckskin enough to graze on for up to several days, if for some reason he was forced to stay here. He could have continued on a while longer. There were still several hours of daylight left before he would be forced to stop for the night, but he dared not chance it. If he did not come upon another such area of grass, he would be forced to backtrack to this place, something he was not prepared to do. It was too difficult to maneuver through once, let alone having to canvas the same place twice.

He broke down his gear and set up his saddle in an overhang of lava. He could make do with the space for the night and he had enough food for several more days. His main concern now was finding enough firewood for a continuous fire.

He set out walking about as the buckskin ignored his departure as he enjoyed his evening graze. It took a considerable amount of time to accumulate enough wood, but he thought he had enough to make it, at least till daylight. It would have to be a small fire, but it would be enough to make his coffee and provide some deterrence of any wild animals that might wander these areas, although he suspected the trappings here for predators would be slim. But a small fire was also a risk, being this close to Lakota land, since they could smell a fire long before they spotted one.

He dropped off the wood and decided to walk about while he still had enough daylight to do so safely. He took his canteen in the hopes that he would come across water.

Going it on foot would take him places that he could not have considered on the back of the buckskin and allow him to see higher up the lava walls and cover more area around him while he could still see. He dared not try to maneuver about after dark. One false move and he could step into a unforgiving pocket or a hole in the lava and seriously injure himself and, like the buckskin, a broken ankle here would seal his fate.

Wandering about also gave him a chance to check out the immediate area without fear that the buckskin would end up in a channel of the lava beds where it could go no further or even turn around. Such a predicament constantly worried Will. He had to be careful where the trail took him. There would be no scaling the walls of the lava if he became trapped. If he wound up in such a situation, he would be forced to back the buckskin out of the trail or watch as the horse became stressed and ended up hurting himself by trying to escape out of sheer panic.

He walked around a curve in the lava and then he came face to face with a recess that had been cut into the rock wall, forcing him to either go under it or over it. He decided on the latter and scaled a short, rather steep wall until he was on top of a small rise. From there, he could see quite a distance around him, something he would never have been able to do from his saddle.

As he looked ahead of him, there was nothing but blackness as far as he could see all the way up to a sheer rock wall directly ahead of him. The land around him had been left brutal by the lava beds. There were no large pockets of grasslands that he could see and nothing but lava for a considerable distance ahead of him and even off to the sides, as well. If there was a canyon hidden here, then it was well protected from searching eyes. Unless someone knew to keep looking for it, they would easily pass by it without even knowing. He wasn't even sure he was in the right vicinity. And even if he were, there would be no way to bring horses out this way. They would have to be taken out another way, or left behind.

He kept an eye on the retreating sun until he felt it best to start back to his camp. He had scouted a good bit and felt more comfortable with where he needed to go from here. Any unnecessary wandering that he could keep the buckskin from being forced into was a good thing.

Will made it back to the camp and had a small fire going by the time the sun slid behind the horizon. It would be cool tonight, but he relished in the fact that at least it wasn't raining. He could only imagine how treacherous maneuvering through these beds would be for his horse if they were slick from rainwater. There would be no escaping injury.

The next morning found him up and moving again after a short breakfast of corn fritters washed down with only a small amount of coffee, since he was having to ration the water remaining in his canteen. The buckskin would need water soon, having received only a limited amount from the dew on the grass and the little he could spare from his canteen.

He was on the trail early, choosing to stir just as the sun began to peek over the mountain range and heat up the lava beds. One thing he had quickly realized was that the sun beating off of the lava could be intense, to say the least. The lava seemed to absorb the sun's heat and was much warmer to the touch than riding over dirt or even rock. He imagined the buckskin was feeling the effects of the heat radiating off the blackened surface, as well. And it was doing nothing to help their need for water.

He was beginning to worry that he had unknowingly subjected the animal to unnecessary stress by bringing him here. He had never imagined the vastness and sparseness of the lava beds and just how brutal the conditions here would be. It was no longer a quest for horses, but one of survival. If they didn't come upon water soon, they would both be in trouble since they would not have enough to make it back to the last collection of water.

His scouting the evening before had provided him with the best path to take for the day. He followed his instincts and started back on the trail to his left, the leg that had branched out a short ways back earlier and looked to be impassable from the ground, but that he had determined was wide enough for the buckskin, anyway.

A large overhang of lava on one side had given him the impression that it could not be traversed, but seeing it from above from when he had scaled the steep wall had confirmed that the turn and the opening had been hidden from the ground, giving the illusion that it was blocked. His backup plan was to backtrack and take the fork to the right, but he had not investigated it enough to be confident he, abad more importantly the buckskin, could make it through. He hated the idea of going back to make the switch to the new trail, but it was only for a short distance and he had convinced himself that it would be worth investigating.

The going was slow, the trail narrow and relentless. The terrain was never changing and though he knew better, it felt as if he were traveling the same path over and over. By mid morning, the heat was already becoming uncomfortable for him. He thought it better to walk again and give the buckskin as much relief as possible.

The constant winding and turns began to feel confusing. He felt as if he had been moving for some time and yet had not gone very far. The constant winding in and around corners was getting annoying as he was burning away his daylight and not getting any closer to finding relief from the lava beds. *How far did they run?* He began to second guess himself and his actions.

As he walked along, he studied the walls of lava around him. In some spots, the lava walls rose five or more feet above where his head would have been had he still been in the saddle. Other times, they were low enough that he could have almost seen over them to the next bend in the trail. But his tracking showed that this had been the way of at least some of the bigger game. There had to be a reason they had traveled this way through this unending maze of passages. If they could make it through there, hopefully he could, too.

The farther he walked, the more he began to become uneasy. For whatever the reason, he did not know. His nagging uneasiness forced him to keep a close eye on the walls above him. There would be no reason for the Lakota to be here, but that wasn't a surety. He was getting deeper into Lakota Territory, but, even so, it didn't mean he would run into them here.

Will continued on, unable to imagine anyone going as far in the lava beds as he had come. Others would have likely abandoned the trek long ago, if they had even entered them to begin with, fearing it would lead them to nothing or, even worse, wind up at a dead-end from which they would have to turn around and retreat back the way they had come. But he wasn't giving up that easily. As long as he could make out the markings of hooves on the lava beds, he would continue moving. Was he chasing a fantasy, one that could easily get him and his horse killed?

He had cornered a rather precarious cleft in the walls when he saw that the trail began to descend. He paused, studying what he could see down it. The trail was still there, and it was a gradual, but steady decline, but it was still hard to see very far down it because of the neighboring blackened walls obscuring some of the natural daylight. The path wasn't overly steep, at least not the part he could see, but it was narrow and fell enough that he felt uncomfortable riding down it. He had only been in the saddle a short distance when he climbed down and took the reins as he started down it, taking his time and looking back randomly to check on the progress of the buckskin.

There were several instances where the horse lost its footing and its feet slid, sometimes almost bringing the animal to its haunches, but each time he was able to recover and keep moving. On one occasion, the buckskin stopped completely, unsure if he wanted to try to continue. But Will felt the animal's hesitation and stopped leading him. He took a moment to speak to the animal while rubbing its jaw and assuring him that it would be okay. Eventually, the buckskin relented and began moving again, once again putting all of his trust in Will.

They continued down the descent, careful to watch the buckskin's steps. After some time, he came upon a sharp corner where one side of the wall jetted out, giving the illusion that it was a dead-end and covering the opening that was concealed beyond it until he happened upon it.

As he rounded the corner, a sparse patch of small trees emerged in front of him, not large enough to conceal any game that might have ventured there and still small enough to remain hidden from those who had not found this scant, almost invisible trail leading down to it. The sight of trees so far down was encouraging to him.

The ground temporarily leveled out as he followed a faint path through the trees and emerged on the other side and into another narrow passage. The cleft between the towering spills of rock began to narrow before he came upon yet another small grove of trees, this one somewhat larger than the first and densely set.

Will carefully traveled through the grove, weaving back and forth. The density of the trees was considerable and its location in the middle of the lava field helped it remain remote. After turning one particular corner, he came upon another cleft in the midst of the sheer wall faces, this one even more narrowed than the previous one. This time, the divide in the rocks was so narrow that he would not be able to ride through it.

He climbed down from the buckskin and led it to the scant opening, glancing up at the sheer walls that enveloped him on either side. He hesitated. Would the buckskin make it through? What if he became wedged and panicked? What good could he do it then? Being trapped would stress the horse too much and could end up killing him.

He started to move and then paused again, wanting to take a look before leading his horse through it, but at the same time, not wanting to leave him behind. He tried to estimate if his horse would fit, but it was simply too close to tell for sure. After a few hesitant moments, he decided to try. He led the buckskin through this last cleft, the sides so narrowed that he had to flip the stirrups over the top of the saddle and, even then, it was uncomfortably

close. The buckskin voiced his displeasure at the
choice, but reluctantly followed Will by passing
through.

They continued heading through the twisting
maze of passages for some time, exactly how long,
Will wasn't sure. He was beginning to worry that his
decision might have cost him the life of his horse
and, in effect, his own. That's when he heard it.

Running water.

It was still faint, but distinct. The sound of
moving water was the first relief he had since
entering the lava beds and encouraged him to keep
going. He had walked the buckskin another fifty feet
when he saw the small waterfall feeding a pool. He
led the buckskin over and both drank their fill. He
was glad to have found water, but that was not what
caught his attention. He was more distracted by the
large valley that lay before him on the other side of
the pool.

The sight of the valley took his breath. It had
once been a volcano which, at one point, had grown
dormant, which explained the presence of the expansive lava bed fields. The rich sediment that was left
behind by the volcano had allowed grass to thrive
here and had transformed the enormous crater into a
canyon of tall, thick grass that blanketed the valley
floor and was greener than any he had ever seen
before.

The valley was spotted with some trees, none of
substantial size, but still large enough to offer some

shelter from the weather. The layout of the canyon explained why the valley had never been discovered before now, since the entire rim of the crater was high and steep enough that no one would have ventured here unless they had a reason to investigate a massive, dormant volcano that would not look dormant from the outside. Anyone passing by would never consider it to be anything that could sustain life. It was perfectly camouflaged.

He walked the buckskin a short distance as he took in the wonders of what nature had naturally created, his enthusiasm and shock of what he was seeing still settling into his mind. It was almost too much to take in and was, to say the least, over-whelming.

As he rode around a small grove of trees, what he saw on the other side stopped him cold. There they were, right in front of him.

Horses.

CHAPTER SIXTEEN

Will Travis couldn't believe his eyes. But there they were. A herd of horses causally grazing in the lush meadow right in front of him. It was almost too good to be true. Some of the horses glanced up at him and then it was as if the entire herd were instantaneously being informed of his presence there. The rest of the herd followed behind them and also glanced his way. Their behavior was that of animals that were probably all wild since they acted as if they had never encountered a human before.

A few of the nearest ones slowly walked in his direction, but only a few feet before stopping and eyeing him carefully. They were in no hurry to come up on this visitor. *Take it easy, Will. They're testing me,* he thought. *Trying to figure out what I am and if I pose a threat to them.*

Will remained motionless. He knew enough about horses to know that becoming accustomed to a new person was a gradual step, especially since they had probably never seen one before. They had spotted the buckskin as one of their own, but were unsure about the thing that sat on its back. He had to be patient and let them accept him only when they were ready. If he tried to advance towards them before they were ready, they would turn and flee and he may never get their trust again or if he did, it could take a considerable amount of time. Time he did not have. He would have to warm up to them slowly and on their terms or risk it taking longer than he had.

Seeing them right here, right then, was overwhelming. He had to take a moment and take it all in. He felt a sense of peace passing over him. A sense of relief. He was happy with himself. For the first time in over a year, he wasn't going to be worried about money. This was his payoff for not giving up, for staying with his goal, and for not letting distractions and obstacles get in his way. Soon, he would have the horses back home and he could use the money he got from selling them and pay everyone he owed and still have enough to save his ranch from foreclosure.

But his celebration was short-lived. It suddenly occurred to him that the reason the horses had not been disturbed wasn't because no one had found them, but possibly because the Lakota had prevented them from doing so. *What if they were watching over them? What if they were watching him right now?*

His first instinct was to wonder if the Lakota

knew he was there. The possibility suddenly kicked him back to reality as worry started overtaking him. He panned the rim of the canyon, looking for movement or any sign that someone was watching him. With the walls of the canyon being so steep and in some places even vertical for several hundred feet or more, it would be difficult for someone to have a vantage point up high enough to see into the canyon and catch someone riding in from the direction of the lava beds. Even if he were spotted, it would take them considerable time to make it all the way down to the valley.

But the longer he thought about it, the more he had to consider the possibility. Would the Lakota put a brave up here day and night, month after month, possibly year after year, just on the off chance that someone made it into the meadow and attempted to take the horses? Granted, it was a far-fetched thought, but not a completely unreasonable one. This was sacred grounds to them, so it was quite plausible, as absurd as it sounded, that they would be willing to guard it so stringently. Besides, if someone were up there, he couldn't imagine where they would be hiding. They would have to be perched way up the wall.

Will climbed down from his saddle and let the buckskin wander a few feet away as it began to engorge itself with the lush, green grass. It was his first step in showing the wild horses that the buckskin was one of them. When the horse had claimed several generous mouthfuls of grass and appeared content for the moment, he slowly walked the buckskin over, nudging him closer to the herd as he looked them over. They were a good, solid stock of colors ranging from white, black and grey to the reddish-brown colored bays. He could tell by the ones closest to him that they had stronger looking legs than a trained, broken horse, another sure sign that they were wild.

He wondered how they had gotten trapped there, and then he realized he had likely answered his own question. At some point, a few wild horses had wandered in here to graze, either by accident, or by being chased by a predator, and had become trapped, quite possibly from an avalanche caused by an unusually heavy rain that had been working away at loose rock for some time and which finally conceded to the elements. With the expansive meadow at their disposal, trees for cover and plenty of water, they found no reason to try to leave this place. Over the years, they had bred and enjoyed a life without the worry of predators, or even humans. It was the ideal setup.

He quickly scanned the herd. By his estimation, there appeared to be upwards of at least sixty head of them. He would have difficulty herding that many horses, but he would worry about that later, depending on how they reacted to him when he got closer to them. For now, he needed to focus all of his attention on finding a way out of the canyon, if there was one.

Will Travis chose a convenient spot under some nearby aspen where he could still keep an eye on the horses who had bedded down for the night, his presence there was not lost on them . After building a fire and eating, he relaxed while he sipped coffee. As he settled into his evening, he watched indirectly as some of the herd eased their way closer to him. Their curiosity was overtaking them to see who this stranger was and why he had appeared in their valley. He made sure not to make any side movements. It was important that he not push making contact with them until they could get accustomed to him. That would make the drive back home much easier for him and them.

This was a good location for him, plenty of game, more than enough fresh water and all the firewood he would possibly ever need. This was a beautiful scene, untouched by man and preserved by nature. It was a tranquil beauty that he would be sorry to leave behind when the time came. Under different circumstances, he could see himself living here, if need be, though he had other plans.

His first night of sleep was not as peaceful as he had hoped. The valley was much cooler at night than he had expected. The dampness of the pooled water caught the persistent breeze that ran through the valley, bringing with it cool chills, forcing Will to unexpectedly feed the fire several times throughout the night.

Morning rang in crisp and quiet. When he opened his eyes, some of the horses were grazing closer to him, which was a good sign. One of them, a rust-colored bay, was particularly curious of Will and nonchalantly grazed right up next to the buckskin. *This must be the lead mare, the alpha mare,* Will thought to himself. *This is the one that will lead the herd. I guess I'll find out when I move them.*

After a quick breakfast, Will decided to gather some more rocks and build a reflective wall on the opposite side of the fire from his bedding to help reflect more heat towards him instead of it being lost in the cooler air.

Will set out to find a way out of the valley. He started with the steep rock walls that enclosed the valley. It would take some time to survey the entire valley, a massive spread, which Will estimated to between two and three miles long and maybe a little more than half as much in width, but he had time on his side, as long as the weather held out. Clouds had been threatening since he had arrived the previous day, but so far, nothing had come of it.

As he scaled the bottom of the sheer rock walls, he came upon large slabs of granite that had broken free at some point from temperature changes contracting and expanding the rock. At this altitude, the temperature here would be quite cold, bringing snow and ice storms with it. Once that moisture settled into the cracks and crevasses, it would freeze in the rigid temperatures and expand, working to loosen the rock until it became free from its foundation and send it cascading downward. He had already come across some pieces of granite much larger than the buckskin that had slid down the wall's face and embedded themselves into the ground.

Above him were even more large slabs, some he estimated weighing upwards of ten tons or more. The sight of such massive sections of rock becoming dislodged was unsettling. He hoped any recent landslides were not cutting off the only route out of the valley. If so, his visit here would end up a miserable failure when he was forced to leave from here without horses.

He spent the remainder of the day searching among the walls connecting to the valley for any sign of access without finding anything of interest. There were simply no routes that could accommodate something as large as a horse. After a day of exhausted searching, he went to bed exhausted, but not defeated. Tomorrow, he would focus his searches on the base of the rock walls for any type of debris that might be standing in his way.

The second day of searching started out as uneventful as the previous one. The only good thing was that some of the horses seemed to be warming up to him. As he traversed the base of the rock walls, some of the horse were moving closer to him, still just out of reach, but letting their curiosity get the better of them. He ignored them, allowing their bravery to grow. They might not have understood what this strange creature was that had invaded their sanitary but, so far, it didn't seem to be a threat of any kind.

On the third day, Will decided to change up his search. He went higher up the walls, off of the valley floor, looking for something that could have hidden a previous trail. Just past midday, he stumbled upon something. It was what looked like an old trail that ascended a few short feet and then disappeared behind a collection of small rocks that had fallen from one of the countless land slides that had occurred here over the years.

He climbed down and released the reins of the buckskin, letting them fall away while the horse directed his attention to the lush grass. Will studied the pile of rocks on top. No one was bigger than his head and could probably be moved by hand. There were some others of larger sizes, but a large limb used as a lever could dislodge them enough to get them rolling down the short incline and moved out of the way, depending on what was on the other side.

He cast a watchful eye on the valley surrounding the buckskin before he scaled over the collection of rocks and landed on the other side, down on an old, forgotten trail. The trail was wide enough to accommodate a horse, in some places possibly even two at once, and headed into a darkened portion of the wall. It ran a few dozen feet through a short cave, carved at some time by the forces of molten lava. The trail was invisible from the valley floor. It had been a miracle that he had even spotted it.

About midpoint of the cave, Will felt a radiating heat coming from the ground. There were small fissures allowing steam to seep through and raising the temperature inside the short cave. The hissing sound emanating from the ground concerned Will. Would it spook the horses? Would it prevent them from even entering the cave? Either of them was quite possible.

He proceeded walking through the cave until he neared the end where he saw daylight coming through the structure. He continued on farther through the rest of the cave and towards the light. When he had traversed the entire length of the cave, he was staring at a wide opening on the lower wall facing that turned into an old game trail. His eyes followed the trail as it began ascending up the wall at a gradual pace, maintaining a comfortable pace that would accommodate a horse, and even a small herd of them.

If he were going to have a chance at getting the horses out of here, it looked like this was his best option.

CHAPTER SEVENTEEN

Will Travis stood and stared at the rocks blocking the path of the trail. He would have to move everything out of the path before a horse would trust it enough to venture inside. But even if the rocks were cleared, would a wild horse be trusting enough to come into a partially enclosed area such as this short cave, especially when they didn't have to be? They could very easily stay put in the wide open, expansive valley rather than risk injury being forced through the bottleneck of a short cave. The only way to see for himself was to clear the way and take the buckskin through. If he could make it, others could follow.

He went to work removing the small rocks by hand and stacked them in a line leading up to the beginning of the trail until he had exhausted himself and had to call it a day as the sun began to slide down past the rim of the valley. Hungry and beaten, Will made a fire and cooked the rabbit he had taken. After devouring the entire thing, he polished off the remains of the coffee he had made and retired to his bedding where he slept straight through till morning, something he had not done in recent memory.

He rose early and, after a quick breakfast, resumed work on the rock pile. The going was tedious but consistent, and by midday, he had removed all the rocks he could physically handle. After some searching, he come upon a small limb that had broken off during a storm and carried it over to the rock pile. He felt as if some of the larger rocks could be moved using the limb as a lever if he could just get it in the right position. He climbed over the small pile of rocks and put the lever to work on the first small boulder.

When he tried to move the first rock, it did not budge. *This was going to be harder than he had imagined.* He made a second attempt, this time prying from a lower spot on the rock. After this failure, he got the idea of placing a small rock under the end of the lever to use as leverage. After some initial failure, the rock began to move. It took a final shift of muscle to move it up and over the remaining pile and send it bouncing off the other rocks and settling on the valley floor. Inspired by this renewed success, he tried his hand at the next rock and dislodged it, as well.

He had found the secret.

After he toiled away at the rocks throughout the remainder of the day, he noticed a gathering of curious horses wanting to investigate what this strange individual was doing in their valley. It was a good sign. His patience at not rushing the herd had paid off. It meant they would be much more receptive to him when the time came to be moved.

The next day, he was back at it, moving the remainder of the rocks that he could pry loose with a lever. It was hot, backbreaking work, but this was the only place he had found that could even possibly be an escape route for the horses. This had been a trail at some point, so there had to be a destination for the animals using it to head to. He was clearing away as many of the smaller rocks as he could. Those that were left over would have to be moved with the help of the buckskin.

He continued to stack the stones he had removed to add to the growing wall that would help channel the horses up and into the cave. Hopefully.

When he had moved everything he could by hand and by lever, it was time to put the buckskin to work. Will hitched his rope around one of the bigger rocks and tied it off to the buckskin. At first, the horse did not move it, but after more coaxing, and him pushing from behind, Will was elated to see the rock moving and finally slide far enough out of the way to fall into the valley. The successful moving of the boulder was encouraging.

Will used his new system to remove two more boulders of equal size as the first before he felt comfortable enough to call it quits. He stood back, admiring his work. Enough rocks had been removed that he was down to dirt. He glanced up the trail and saw nothing that should overly concern the horses. The only part of the route that he was worried about was the steam rising through the fissures, and he had a plan for that. He took some branches from a fallen tree and laid them across the opening of the path to keep the horses from possibly venturing there on their own.

Will then went to work collecting small branches and throwing them on top of the fissure until no more steam could be seen or heard. They would still absorb the heat, but it would help lower the temperature inside the cave and it would cover up anything coming up from the ground.

After sufficiently covering the fissure, all that was left now was to herd the horses onto the trail and convince them to follow it up the side of the canyon.

He had walked a short distance on the trail on the other side of the cave and had found nothing else blocking its path. It looked as if the rest of the trail would be open for them to pass thorough.

Thoroughly exhausted, he set out to head back to his camp, where he ate and enjoyed his coffee as the sun went down behind the canyon face. He would try to herd some of the horses tomorrow to get a feel of how cooperative they would be. Right now, he needed sleep.

. . .

The coolness of the morning, coupled with the absence of a working fire, caused Will to rise and get started with his day sooner than he expected. After a quick breakfast, he saddled the buckskin and rode over to where the herd had migrated most recently.

He rode around behind them and began yelling and swinging his rope to get their attention. At first, the lead mare was not interested in doing as he bid, but after more coaxing, she finally took off at a slow trot with others filing in and following behind.

Will corralled the horses for a short distance, starting out with only ten horses to see how well he could manage them. He would have to start out slow since he didn't know how many he was going to be able to bring with him when he left. He would try a larger herd next and see how well that went. If it turned out to be too many, he would have to find an amount that he felt he could easily manage.

The ten horses ran well together, and he was relieved to see that he was able to steer them where he wanted. He circled around and picked up ten more, joining them up with the first group and running them down the valley towards the trail, but stopping a short distance from it. He didn't want to introduce them to the trail until it was time for them to leave.

The horses seemed right at ease with his presence, which was a welcome relief for him. With their easy temperament, he should be able to move them relatively easily.

By midday, he noticed that dark, threatening clouds had begun to form in the south and were moving in his direction. This was not good news. He had been concerned about the steepness and stability of the trail leading out of there under dry conditions. How much more treacherous would the trail become after a torrential downpour? With so much rock surrounding them, the trail would become slippery and could take considerable time to dry out enough to safely move the horses.

He had to get the herd moving.

Will left the herd and rode back to the beginning of the trail. He believed there were enough rocks carefully laid out to funnel the horses onto the trail, but he needed to make sure. If they ran past it the first time, it would be even more difficult and take more time to drive them through there the second time. And with the advancing storm, it was time he did not have.

He collected more limbs and placed them in a curve farther down from the opening to persuade the horses to take the trail. Since they had been born and raised here, he worried they would be hesitant to leave the expansive valley, the only place they were familiar with and had ever known as home, and head down a narrow trail, but at least he had to try. If he could just get the lead mare on it, the others were sure to follow.

Will stood back and looked over his work. It would have to do. It was the best he could do with the limited amount of time he had. Moving the rocks had taken longer than he had anticipated. All that was left now was to get the herd pointed in that direction.

He cast a glance over to the south. The storm was building. By the looks of it, and from his experience being caught on the side of the mountain coming there, he had only a few hours to get the herd moving up the trail. They had to reach a point where they could bed down for the night and ride out the storm. If he could just convince the herd to go up the trail, they would continue moving until they stopped at the first opening that gave them water and grass to graze on, assuming he could convince them of such.

He jumped into the saddle and took off for the herd, which had migrated closer to the trail. He wasn't hung up on numbers anymore. He would drive the herd towards the trail and whatever number of horses he ended up going in that direction would be what he would take. There would be no time for a second pass.

As he rode closer to them, part of the herd at the rear broke off and headed in the opposite direction, carrying two foals with them. He split between the two groups and looped around, driving as many horses as he could forward. The lead mare took charge and took the herd down towards the trail, with Will bringing up the rear. He was careful not to push them too quickly for fear that they would pass the opening, leaving him with having to start herding them all over again.

The lead mare continued down the valley at a brisk pace, but not at too fast of a pace that it would run past the trail. As they got closer, Will held his breath with the hope that she would take the turn as he had laid it out and start up the trail.

He backed off from driving them to allow them to slow down on their own to make the turn. Would it be enough?

As the lead mare came up to the opening, she seemed a bit confused at first, perhaps because she had never seen this opening before. She seemed to hesitate only for a split second, but then she turned and started up the trail, bringing the others filling in behind her.

Will pulled back and allowed the horses to enter the trail without his prodding. He watched every one of them line up and enter without delay until the last one was directly in front of him, awaiting their turn. He brought up the rear, following the last one headed up the trail. He could not see the whereabouts of the lead mare, but since the herd's movement had not stalled, he had to assume she was continuing up the trail.

Right before he disappeared into the shallow, short cave at the trail entrance, he cast one final glance at the valley he was leaving with a mixture of sadness and relief. The sadness was for the ones left behind who would wonder what had happened to the others. They would have the choice of leaving on their own, should they develop the courage to do so, provided another landslide didn't occur before they made up their mind, or they could stay behind and live out their lives as they were now living. The relief was from what he expected to get for the ones he was now driving. It would easily be enough to save him and his ranch.

For the first time in a very long time, he felt optimistic about his future.

CHAPTER EIGHTEEN

Will followed the herd for almost an hour, steadily climbing at a slight, gradual incline the entire time. The trail was better than he had expected and had proven to be more than adequate to move the horses through. So far, there had been no obstacles or interruptions to slow the movement of the herd. His hope was that the herd would stop at the first sign of either water or grass, allowing him time to catch up with the lead mare and see what progress they had made getting out of the canyon.

Over the next half-hour, he stopped twice at breaks in the trees to glance back at the approaching storm. Judging from the dampness of the air and the lowered temperature being pushed by the storm, it would be upon them soon, probably within the next half hour, maybe less. They needed to get to more level ground before then. They were still moving when the first of the rain began to fall. Within a minute, it had turned into a significant rainstorm.

Will tilted his hat to help shield his face from the stinging rain while keeping a close eye on the trail. The ascent was still gradual, but he still worried about how slippery the rocks underneath the hooves of the horses would be. He would use the buckskin to help determine if the going became too treacherous. But as long as the herd kept moving, so would he.

After a brief shower, the rain started to dissipate and the dark sky began parting and allowing the sun to peer through in limited amounts. He welcomed the end of the storm. Judging from the location of the sun, he estimated he had only a couple of hours of daylight left. But, so far, the herd had not stopped.

Another half-hour passed and still the herd continued moving. He passed several spots on the trail that offered some grass, but not enough to sufficiently feed the herd. Will had started to worry. What if they did not make it to a large enough clearing before nightfall? What then? What if the lead mare got confused and decided to head back down the mountain? He wouldn't be able to stop a herd of horses coming down at him.

He was running out of time when the movement of the herd slower down considerably. He continued moving until the trail leveled out into a large plateau with a small patch of tall, lush grass and several pockets in the rocks that had collected rainwater.

The area wasn't overly large in size, but it would be enough for the horses to get their fill for the night.

Will dismounted and tied the buckskin off on a picket line he had strung across the trail leading downward to block their retreat. As the horses busied themselves gorging on the thick grass, Will immediately went to work collecting the few fallen limbs that he could find to help block their back trail and in front to contain the horses overnight before he also collected a few rocks to contain a small campfire.

After eating, Will took his cup of coffee and casually walked around the herd as they lounged about in their unfamiliar surroundings, making sure to remain a safe distance behind them so as not to spook them. It was the first opportunity he had to count the number of horses he was able to remove. After checking and rechecking his numbers, he settled on the number of twenty-seven, which was more than he had anticipated and a welcome surprise.

Will also surveyed the trail leading upward. After the plateau where they had stopped, the trail opened up more and wasn't as steep as what they had already traversed, which was a good sign and meant that they could make better time once they left in the morning. His guess was that they would be up and over the rim of the canyon and onto the prairie early tomorrow, depending on how steep and crowded the trail was from here on. Regardless of what he came upon from after this, it was still better than the journey into the valley.

The following morning, Will was up and eager to finish the stretch to the top of the canyon and out onto the open prairie. After breaking down his camp and taking down his simple blockade in the front, he climbed into the saddle and started the horses up the remainder of the trail. In just a few minutes, they had finally surfaced on the prairie, a welcome sight to him and, he believed, the horses, too.

Now that they were finally on level ground, the lead mare took off. It was all the buckskin could do to keep up the wild horses as it ran up on their sides to contain them as much as possible, while continuing to head them in the right direction.

Will had some experience with herding horses, but nothing could have prepared him for this. These horses were wild and spirited, anxious to be on the move. They followed the lead horse, who didn't hold anything back. She was as free as any animal he had ever encountered and loved to show it.

As the morning faded away, Will turned to glance behind him and was suddenly conscious of the dark clouds forming behind him. It was another rainstorm approaching, but this one differed from the one he had encountered the day before. This one covered a more expansive portion of the sky and judging from the blackness of the clouds, it was going to be brutal.

He had no choice but to push the herd onward, using the openness of the valley to speed their retreat from the upcoming weather. Another hour later, the temperature of the air dropped considerably in a short amount of time as moisture replaced the dry heat. Once it began to rain, it did so with a vengeance. Although Will did not care to work in the rain, he was still relieved that this larger, worse storm had not hit them on the side of the mountain.

Will rode up alongside the lead mare several times to check her direction and was satisfied that she was still heading where they needed to go. The rain had not let up and was slowing their movements, but as long as they continued forward, he saw no need to push them.

It wasn't long before the storm fizzled out and the sun returned. The herd continued moving at a steady pace until it got late enough in the evening to stop for the night. Will picked a small indentation in the wall of the mountain to stop. There was ample grass here and a small creek. The horses would be fine here for the night. Will made his fire in front of the horses to help persuade them to stay put.

The herd was moving early the next morning and traveled over the following day without incident. During that time, Will had encountered no one, which was what he hoped for. He didn't want to have to explain where he had acquired a herd of wild horses, nor did he want to risk someone trying to take them from him.

On the second day, a thunderstorm appeared seemingly out of nowhere, catching the herd out in the open. Will considered finding a place to hole up and wait it out, but there was nowhere in sight that looked like it would be sufficient, so he decided to continue on until they came across something.

Will tried to take in his surroundings to determine exactly where they were. He thought they were out of Lakota Territory and heading to the outskirts of Hangman's Gulch, which he would go around, but with the rain shading everything, he couldn't be sure. He was still pondering his location when the bullet stripped the skin from the side of his head, just above his eye and back across his temple and beyond.

The impact of the bullet pulled his head around partially to the side, as if he had been kicked by a mule. He suddenly felt woozy and disoriented, but he tried to gather his senses enough to continue riding. His head throbbed fiercely, and his sight was distorted from the impact of the bullet and the blood running freely down into his right eye. His head wavered for only a few seconds longer before he lost his balance and fell from his horse into the mud.

Will landed in the mud on his back, stunned and motionless. He tried to get up, but his head was so disoriented he couldn't get his brain to process what needed to be done to do so. He thought of drawing his gun, but he would have no luck taking aim, even if he somehow managed to get it out of its holster. Besides, any type of movement would give away the fact that he was still alive. Whoever had shot him might believe him already dead. If he showed signs that he was still alive, they would more than likely finish him off.

He laid with the rain pelting his face and obscuring his view while a rider approached. Out of the corner of his eye, he saw a horse ride up and stop just a few yards away from where he lay. He closed his eyes and tried not to move, despite the intense pain in his head.

The rider never got down from their saddle as a second horse rode up beside him. "Hey, will you look at that? That's the same guy we caught before," the first man stated.

"Yeah, it sure is. I wondered what happened to him."

"Look. I nearly took the side of his head off with that shot," the first man said proudly.

"You sure did," the second man agreed with a soft chuckle. "That was some good shooting, Russ, considering it's raining."

"And I wasn't even aiming for his head."

"Then you got lucky."

"I guess so, but what do we do with him?"

"You heard what Bell said. Kill him the next time we saw him and it looks like you did, but I ain't dragging him all the way back to camp for nothing. Bell will just have to take our word for it."

"I knew he was stupid," the first man said as he stared down at Will, "but I never thought he'd show his face around here again."

"Not and bring a herd of horses with him. Wonder where he got these?"

"Don't none of them have a brand. They look to be wild."

"Now, where would he get a herd of wild horses?"

"I dunno, but we'd better get 'em over to Bell before he wonders where we are."

The second man scoffed out loud. "He ain't gonna care where we were when he sees what we brung him. I wonder where that indian that let him go is?'

"I dunno, but I'd love to get my hands on him for killing Miles."

"Well, c'mon. We got to stay with these horses."

Will remained still as he heard the two men climb into their saddles and ride away, running the horses with them. *His* horses. The horses *he* had worked so hard to bring back to save his future. Now they were gone. And to make it worse, it was by the likes of Bell and his men. But as much as it pained him to think about his loss, his first priority was to get out from the open and into some type of shelter before nightfall. Laying out here, exposed, bleeding, helpless. He wouldn't make it till morning.

He tried to lift his body from the mud, but his head and his limbs were not cooperating with one another. He had a headache unlike any before, and even the rain was stinging the side of his head when it made contact. He continued to struggle until his head fell back into the mud and he passed out.

He woke up briefly, startled by a sound that he

couldn't quite make out. At first, he thought it was someone talking, but their words were jumbled and made no sense to him. He tried to call out to them, but his head hurt too much to try to concentrate.

He blacked out.

It was still raining when Will dreamed he was being lifted out of the mud and placed across a horse. He tried to open his eyes, but the combination of mud and blood that was smeared across his face was obstructing his vision. He tried to sit up, but was forcibly pushed back down again by the rider's hand. When he reached up and felt the side of his head, his hand was quickly pulled away. It was then that he realized this wasn't a dream.

Someone had him.

Will tried to speak, but his head was still so disoriented that he lacked the willpower to fight through the pain and dizziness enough to form words. Whoever had him, was not interested in hearing anything from him. Who were they? Why had they brought him with them? Where were they going? Why had they not finished him off?

He passed out again before he could get his answers.

CHAPTER NINETEEN

Will's eyes opened slowly.

His level of pain was not as severe as the last time he had opened his eyes. When was that? When he had been shot?

It took a few seconds for his eyesight to focus. The first thing he realized was that it was no longer raining. The second thing was that he had no idea where he was.

He was looking around, taking in the fact that he was inside what looked to be a teepee, when he tried to move his hands and discovered that they were tied, as were his feet. Why was he in restraints? Could they not see that he was not a threat in his condition?

He caught a glimpse of a young boy who had been sitting quietly across the fire from him. When he began stirring, the young boy jumped up and ran outside. Will tried to sit up, but his head was pounding relentlessly and it felt better to lie back down. His head felt as it were bound by something. When he tried to reach up, he could not feel the bandage wrapped around his head, although he realized what it was. It was only a brief time later that the flap of the teepee opened and two Lakotas walked in. The older of the two sat across from him where the boy had been sitting, while the younger one sat next to him. Will tried to get a good look at the two men, but his eyesight was still a little hazy. The older brave spoke first. Will could not understand him.

Two Elk (Lakota) "........... ... ."

Will gathered that the young Lakota was the translator. The younger Lakota held up his hand holding the necklace that Walks With Horse had given him after he had helped the old Indian back at the trading post. The translator's eyes were stern and fixed on Will. "Where did you get this necklace?"

The sight of the necklace caused Will to look down to verify that it was his necklace that had once hung around his neck. His delay in answering irritated the young Lakota.

"Tell me. Where did you get it?" He asked again, this time more forcefully.

"Why am I tied up?" Will asked as he tested the bonds that held his hands out in front of him.

"Answer the question."

"Untie me and I will."

"No. You will answer our questions before your hands and feet are freed."

"I've done nothing wrong. I'm not answering anything."

"Then you will remain tied up until you do."

Will sighed heavily, his anger starting to build before he began. "An old man gave it to me."

"What old man?"

"A Lakota."

"What is his name?"

"Walks With Horse."

The young brave turned to the older man and spoke. After the older brave answered him, the younger brave looked back at Will.

"Why did he give it to you?" The young brave asked.

"No more questions until I get some answers of my own. To start with, who are you? And who is he?" Will asked as he nodded towards the older man.

"He is Two Elk, chief of this tribe, and I am Laughing Otter."

"How did you find me?"

"What is your name?"

"How did you find me?"

"Tell me your name first."

"Will Travis."

"Well, Will Travis, one of our braves saw your horse and then found you lying out in the open. He would have taken your horse and weapons and left you there, but he saw your necklace was of Lakota, and he brought you here. That necklace is the only thing that saved you."

"Why am I tied up?"

"Because we did not know what type of man you were, if your heart was pure or evil. We had to make sure before the choice for you to be set free in our camp."

"Where did you learn to speak English so well?"

"I was stationed at Fort Kellum after the war. I learned English from one of the women who taught the children of the fort. Now, you will answer my questions. Why did Walks With Horse give you this necklace? He would not part with it unless it was for good reason."

"I helped him out with some men who were trying to attack him and I gave him a blanket and some food and a place to sleep."

"Why were you nice to Walks With Horse? It is not normal. White man does not help Lakota."

"He needed my help, and he was hungry and cold. It was the right thing to do. Did you know he was sick?"

"Yes," Laughing Otter answered, although hesitantly. "He is very sick. Not getting better. Medicine man try, but cannot help him. Walks With Horse once great warrior. But now, he has been sick for some time from white man disease," the young Lakota responded. "As long as Walks With Horse remains sick, cannot come back again."

Will now knew that Laughing Otter was referring to Walks With Horse's illness as being tuberculosis. "When he came here, he made other Lakota sick, didn't he? That's why he can't come back here again, isn't it?"

"Yes." Laughing Otter turned and relayed the story to Two Elk. Two Elk responded while he pointed at Will.

"Two Elk wants to know why you were on Lakota land. You are not welcome here, even if you did help Walks With Horse."

"I was looking for something."

Laughing Otter looked at him with curiosity. "What were you looking for?"

Will shook his head in disgrace. "It doesn't matter. It's gone now."

"You were looking for Kawnteenowah."

The mention of the name spurred a reaction from Will, causing him to glance over at Laughing Otter. Though he remained silent, his expression gave away his guilt.

Laughing Otter studied Will carefully. "Kawnteenowah. You know this name, do you not?"

Will considered lying to them, but he didn't know what they would do to him when they found out and all they would have to do was to send a brave into the valley and see where he had stolen the horses and how he had gotten them out of there. Since the horses were gone from his possession, he had nothing to lose by telling them the truth.

"Do you not know this name, Will Travis?" Laughing Otter pushed him for an answer.

Will's head hung a little from his guilt. "Yes. I know it."

"Did you take horses from Kawnteenowah?"

Again, Will felt reluctant to admit it. If they were going to kill him, then they would do it regardless of if he told the truth. "Yes," he said sheepishly.

"How many horses did you take, Will Travis?"

"Twenty seven."

Laughing Otter's reaction to the number was not a good one. He spoke to Two Elk. When the old man answered him, Laughing Otter told Will what he said. "What did you do with these horses?"

Will was almost too embarrassed to answer him. "I was taking them back home to sell. I needed the money. I'm sorry. I wasn't trying to disturb your valley. I just didn't have any other choice."

"White man is not welcome in Kawnteenowah. Valley only for Lakota. Horses are sacred and only for warriors who are passing into the spirit world. Bad medicine goes to those who should not go there. Lakota law say anyone who goes there will be killed for disturbing sacred land and taking horses."

"I know I wasn't supposed to go in there, but I was desperate. I owe a lot of money and this was the only way to get the money I needed."

"It is Lakota law that no one go into Valley of Horses. You are not to disturb the valley where ancient ones put horses. Now you have taken horses from warriors who deserve them when they leave to go on into the spirit world."

"I'm sorry," Will said solemnly again. "I was desperate. I didn't know what else to do."

"Did you tell anyone else of Kawnteenowah?"

"No. I'm the only one who knows."

"Was anyone else with you?"

"No. I did it alone."

"Doe anyone else know how to get to Kawn-teenowah?"

"No. I found it by accident."

"Lakota law say you must die since you have gone there and taken some of the horses."

"Isn't there something I can do to make this right? I didn't mean to cause any problems. I just needed those horses."

"Our law is clear and not to be broken."

Will looked up at Laughing Otter. "What if I could replace them? Would you consider allowing me to live?"

"How will you replace them when you do not know where they are? There are no tracks to follow. Rain washed them away."

"You don't need tracks," Will stated firmly, remembering the man who shot him had talked of Bell, the leader of the men in Hangman's Gulch who had taken him prisoner and tried to kill him. "I know where they are."

"How can you be sure?"

"Because I know the men who shot me and took them away from me."

Laughing Otter spoke to Two Elk, who responded

back in Lakota.

"Two Elk say you are honorable man for helping Walks With Horse without cause. Most would not do so. He says it shows you have good, decent heart. Because you save Walks With Horse, if you return horses you took, you may live. Where are horses?"

"Hangman's Gulch. Have you heard of it?"

"Yes," Laughing Otter answered. "We know of such a place. Many bad men there. Men who kill Lakota for no reason. Many braves have been lost to these bad men." Will heard the anger in Laughing Otter's voice.

"I'll go there and get your horses back. I promise." Will proclaimed. "I got caught up in my own problem. I made a mistake, I understand that now, and I'm sorry, but I need a chance to make this right. If you'll give me that chance, I'll get them back."

After confirming with Two Elk, Laughing Otter nodded in agreement. "Good, Will Travis," he spoke as he stood and walked over, pulling a knife from his waist as he did. Will tensed up, fearing the man would attack him for his actions. Instead, he leaned down and held Will's hands steady as he cut the rope from them. He did the same to free Will's legs before looking back at Will. "You will go and get back horses, Will Travis," he said as he sheathed his knife before looking back at him. "And we will go with you."

.   .   .

The man named Bell was in the cave, impatiently riding out the storm when he heard them coming. Even over the rain, he knew enough to know the distinct sound of hooves smashing into the ground. This was not as thundering as a herd of cattle, but it was along the same lines. *Was it a rider? No, not even multiple riders. This was something more*.

He walked over to the edge of the cave to glance out into the area where the corral containing their horses was located when he saw them round the last corner and come into the clearing. Horses. But not just everyday horses. He could tell by their demeanor that they were not only wild, but some of the most perfect, well-developed animals he had ever seen. The group was led by two of his men, Dawson bringing up the side, followed by Friedman bringing up the rear. Bell watched them run the stock into the corral and secure them as he waited inside the dryness of the cave until both men walked over.

"What d'ya think, Bell?" Dawson asked with a proud smile as he shook his hat to relieve it of water.

"Where did *they* come from?" Bell asked with interest.

"You're never going to believe this, but we got 'em off that drifter that got away a few days ago, when Miles was killed."

The news shocked Bell. "*Him?* You got these from *him?* Where did *he* get 'em?"

Friedman answered. "Don't know."

"I *knew* there was something going on with him,"

Bell exclaimed. "I *knew* he was lying to us. So what happened?"

"We were riding back from hunting when we got caught out in a rainstorm that snuck up on us. We didn't have any place to hole up, so we just kept riding to get back here," he said as he nodded at the other man. "He saw somebody coming with these horses, but from where we were positioned, they couldn't see us. He got off a shot and almost took the man's head off. When we rode down to check on him, we saw that it was that drifter fella."

"Was he alone?" Bell asked, his enthusiasm building. "He didn't happen to have that Indian with him, did he?"

Friedman shook his head. "Nah. He was alone."

"That's too bad," Bell said in a disappointing tone. "I'd love for you to have killed that Indian, too, for what he did to Miles. And I'd still like to know where that drifter got those wild horses."

"I dunno," Dawson added, "but those are some of the best stock I've ever seen."

Bell tossed the remnants of his coffee and sat down his cup. "You fellas get some rest. Renslow and Arturo will be here sometime tomorrow with the cattle they took. We'll put them with the horses and take 'em all down to Plainville once this weather clears up."

CHAPTER TWENTY

Will spent the rest of the day moving about and trying to regain his senses while he prepared to leave. His head was still hurting, but the Lakota had given him some type of medicinal drink that was so horrible that he imagined it would be what used bathwater must taste like. Still, it had helped him feel much better, considering his injury. His unsteady legs had also gotten better.

As he laid in his bed resting, a young Lakota woman came in with a fresh bandage and a bowl of some type of mixture. Her features were striking, and he could not help but stare at her. She said nothing as she motioned for him to lie down on his back. When he complied, she unwrapped the bandage and laid it off to the side. Will caught a glimpse of it and saw blackened, dried blood covering the inside of it.

The young Lakota woman turned Will's head back forward so she could treat his wound. As she mixed up the contents of the bowl with a wooden spoon, Will took the opportunity to feel his wound. His fingers carefully traced the side of his head right above his eye where the bullet had creased him. The wound was deep, all the way through to the bone, and he could feel his skull. If the bullet had been just a slight bit closer, it would have gone into his skull instead of scraping across it. He had been exceptionally lucky. He would likely have a horrific scar for the rest of his life.

Will lay still while the young Lakota woman smeared the mixture onto his wound. As soon as it made contact, he felt a burning sensation that felt as if his skin were immediately on fire. The sensation also felt as if it were creeping into his head. He pulled her hand back from applying more of the mixture as he seethed from the burning. He had not realized that Laughing Otter had slipped into the teepee at some point unnoticed until he heard him speak.

"You must allow her to put medicine on your wound," Laughing Otter announced. "It is only thing that will help it heal and not become infected."

"It burns too much," Will stated as he continued to hold on to her arm. She tried to pull free, but he would not let go of her. She turned to Laughing Otter and spoke.

"What did she say?" Will asked.

"She said if you don't let her finish, she will call braves in here to hold you down."

Will looked back at the young woman as stared

back at him and waited for his response. She was not backing down from her duties, so with the threat of being held down, Will released her arm and allowed her to finish. She continued to cast glimpses at him while she worked until she had placed the new bandage on his head. As she gathered her things to leave, he touched her arm gently, drawing her attention. "Can you tell her I said thank you?" Laughing Otter relayed his message and the young Lakota woman cast a smile at Will before she left the teepee.

Will wanted to get used to being on his feet again to test his steadiness now that they were going up against Bella and his men. He also worried about being in the saddle and all the movement that came with it. If he could not ride, he could not lead the Lakota to their horses. By the time he could, the horses were sure to be long gone.

He stepped outside, taking in both the activity of the camp and the weather at the same time. No one paid him an overly amount of attention, no doubt because of orders from Two Elk. That did not prevent him from receiving judgements glares from the tribes people. He could tell by the looks on their faces that they had heard what he had done and were disgusted by it. He wanted to tell them that it was a mistake and that he was ashamed of his actions, but he knew they would not believe him. His only proof was to bring the horses back to them.

As he walked about the Lakota, he came across the young woman who had bandaged his head. He gave her an awkward, harmless smile, which she returned before she was summoned back to her duties by an older woman who was in charge of over-seeing the young woman's work.

He had finally wandered the confines of the camp and ended up with the horses. To his surprise, he was glad to see the Lakota warrior that had found him on the prairie had also found his beloved buckskin. He had been heartbroken, thinking he had lost his friend since he assumed he would never see his horse again. After a short, joyous reunion with the animal, he packed his saddlebags with provisions from the Lakota camp and readied for his departure at first light.

He was walking back from where the horses were tied off when he caught a glimpse of someone off in the edge of the thicket. His reaction was to turn to see who it was as he went for his revolver, only to remember that his gun had been taken from him when he arrived in the Lakota camp. He glanced back and thought he saw Walks With Horse disappearing into the woods, but when he turned to get a better look, the man was gone.

Early the next morning, when Will emerged from his teepee, he saw Laughing Otter and some of the other braves were already mounting their horses, as if they were preparing to leave. He thought of asking about Walks With Horse, but decided there was no need to draw attention to the old man. If it had been him, his presence there would have been hard to explain since he was removed from the tribe for having tuberculosis. Will walked over to Laughing Otter, putting Walks With Horse out of his mind for the time being, more confused by the display of the braves.

"Where are all of you headed?" Will asked as he scanned the number of braves who had obviously readied for a trip.

"We're going with you, Travis, but only up to the edge of Lakota land. We do not travel into land of bad men. Too many Lakota would be killed for nothing. We will wait at the edge of Lakota land while you bring horses back to us."

"But I thought you were going *with* me to get the horses back."

Laughing Otter shook his head with a deadpan look. "Two Elk did not like that plan. He says it's too dangerous for Lakota to go onto bad man land," he insisted. "Instead, we will wait in valley, on Lakota land, for you to return with the horses."

Will scoffed out loud at his predicament. He had anticipated the Lakota going in with him. Now, as it stood, it would be one gun against Bell and all of his men. He had no reason to believe that he could make it out of there alive, even without the horses.

He quickly saddled the buckskin and a short time later, the group quietly left the Lakota camp in single file fashion with Will and Laughing Otter riding side-by-side in the lead.

They traveled the day, the entire group quiet and

calm. Will was amazed at just how quiet the Lakota moved about. They were disciplined and well trained, to say the least. It was how they hunted elk, buffalo, or any other game. Hunting men was no different. There was no talking amongst them. No need for words. They knew what needed to be done and were prepared to do it, and whatever else was necessary.

They bedded down and went about setting up their camp with the efficiency that he had grown to admire. The braves readied their weapons and painted their horses in preparation for riding them into battle. As everyone sat down with their evening meal, Will was left to eat in private. He did not know if that was because of his part in bringing them here to have to recover what was rightfully theirs, or if he had been excluded from the preparation because he was not Lakota. Either way, the despondent looks thrown his way throughout the meal told him that he was the topic of their conversation.

By Will's estimation, it was another half-day's ride to Hangman's Gulch. Despite the presence of the tribe and considering how his last encounter had ended, he had a certain uneasiness at the thought of going back there.

Judging from the expressions on the faces of his Lakota friends, they did not.

The sunrise of the following morning came with the Lakota already on their feet and breaking down their camp. Little was spoken as they moved about and within the half hour, they were on the trail again.

The Lakota party was eight men strong. Will had no idea just how many men were under Bell's command, nor did he know how many other men were hiding out there that were not affiliated in any way with Bell. When Bell took him hostage, he had spoken of there being others, but Will had never seen or heard of others and he and Walks With Horse had not encountered others when they escaped. He was beginning to wonder if Bell was lying about his numbers, exaggerating them in an attempt just to keep others away.

As they rode, Will wondered what would happen if the herd was no longer in Bell's possession. He supposed he would be killed, not that he didn't deserve it. The only thing saving him thus far was his involvement in recovering the horses. If he was no longer able to do that, there would be no need to spare him and his life would not be worth saving. He would be killed and he would have no one to blame but himself.

They had lost an entire day from the time the Lakota had found him out on the prairie till now. The weather had been miserable when he had been shot, a fact that Will hoped had worked to their advantage. Bell would likely not have wanted to run a herd of wild horses in such bad weather and would probably have chosen to wait out the storm. That would put them almost a half-day behind Bell and the herd, if they had left right away. From the course they were on, Laughing Otter had apparently taken that into consideration.

"Those who took the horses must travel to the south to sell them," Laughing Otter spoke during a brief stop. "You must catch up to them before they get horses to town."

"How am I supposed to get into Hangman's Gulch and get back out alive with the horses?"

"This is not Two Elk's problem, nor is it mine. This is not our fight. Bad men wait inside there to shoot Lakota. We would lose too many braves. The Lakota are safer on Lakota land. Travis, you will go in there and bring the horses back to us. Only then will you will be free to leave."

Will understood Laughing Otter's concern. This wasn't their fight. The only reason they were even there was because they had been pulled into this because of his actions and they were not interested in losing men because of him. Two Elk and Laughing Otter did not expect him to make it out of there alive, but they certainly weren't going to let innocent braves get slaughtered, either.

If he tried to confront Bell inside the Gulch, Bell would have the advantage. His life would be sacrificed before they could even get close to Bell. His best bet was to catch them out in the open, where he would have more of an advantage. If Bell had not left with the herd before now, he would have no other choice but to go in there and get them.

Besides retrieving the herd, there were other

reasons why the Lakota had a special hatred for the men who inhabited Hangman's Gulch. When Laughing Otter found out where the horses had likely been taken, he told Will of several instances where Lakota had ventured close to the place and had been killed by the bad men there, for no other reason but than to brag about killing them. Two Elk had stepped in and prohibited anyone from the tribe of going near there. Will knew Laughing Otter would revel in the opportunity of getting revenge for the senseless loss of his tribal brothers, but that revenge would not be exacted today.

They rode for another hour with no sign of the herd, cutting across the vastness of the prairie and heading southwest to intercept Bell below Hangman's Gulch in the event that he had already left. Laughing Otter was taking a huge risk by assuming the horses would be carried south to be sold, but Will felt it was a risk he was not willing to interfere with.

It would make no sense to keep the horses in Hangman's Gulch since there were no substantial grazing areas to support so many of them. Besides, Bell would be more interested in getting rid of them as soon as possible and pocketing the money. For all Bell knew, those horses belonged to Will. And even if Will was the rightful owner, there was still the possibility that other men held a percentage of the interest in them. Because of that risk, Bell would not be interested in having them in his possession if the rightful owner gathered the nerve to come looking for them. Bell still believed in the secrecy and intimidation of his hideout, but with that many head of wild horses, it would be worthwhile for others, meaning their rightful owners, to come looking for them.

It was midmorning when Laughing Otter held up his hand to stop their movement as he continued to lock his eyes on a point in the distance in front of them. Will stopped alongside him and followed his line of sight to a spot just before the crest of the mountains.

"This is the edge of Lakota land," he advised Will. "You will go the rest of the way."

Will started not to question Laughing Otter's actions, but his curiosity was too great. "If you were planning to send me in there alone all along, then why even bother coming this far?"

"Even though you helped Walks With Horse, Two Elk not trust white man, not even you, Will Travis. He is afraid you'll get the horses and not bring them back. We are here to make sure you do."

Will opened his mouth to defend himself, but then decided his actions had sealed Two Elk's opinion of him. It was a suicide mission, and he had put himself in this position. If, by some miracle, he somehow managed to retrieve the horses, he would return them to the Lakota and go back home only to lose everything, but at least his life would be spared. If he were caught, he was a dead man. If he decided not to try to made a run for it, the Lakota would track him down and kill him, no matter where he ended up. Any way he tried, he ended up with the short end of the deal. He had no other choice but to sneak into Hangman's Gulch and try to find those horses.

With any luck, they would still be there.

CHAPTER TWENTY-ONE

Bell sipped his coffee while he waited, looking favorably out over the corral full of wild horses. It was like Dawson had said. They were the best stock he had ever laid eyes on. They would bring good money just as soon as they could get them to town.

The great thing about selling wild horses was that there was no brand to have to alter. There was no previous owner to contend with. No explanation as to how they were acquired or where they came from was necessary. And they were guaranteed to bring a substantial windfall of money. It was the perfect scenario, and he didn't even have to round them up. The drifter he had captured had done that for him.

Along with the twenty-seven horses they had taken from Will, there was also almost a hundred head of cattle that some of his men had stolen from one of the prominent ranches just west of Hangman's

Gulch that had just arrived. They would set out for Plainville at first light.

Now that the cattle had arrived, Bell felt confident about their trip to Plainville. His men had stormed the Sliding J Ranch just before dawn the previous night and had taken the majority of the ranch's herd, killing the owner and his three ranch hands in the process when they tried to stop them. One of the ranch hands had stayed alive long enough for the sheriff to hear who was responsible.

The Sliding J was not a large ranch and with only the four men working it, did not have the men to go after Bell and his gang. Instead, the neighboring ranches had reached out to the local authorities for protection. But once word spread that Bell was the one who had raided the ranch, the local authorities quickly found reason to lose interest in pursuing them. With no remaining heirs to the Sliding J, the raid went unpunished. Once again, as expected, Bell's notoriety had paid off. He was contemplating the next move after selling off the herds when one of his men, Jed Castle, walked up to him.

"How's the herd?" Bell inquired of the man.

"Pretty quiet," Castle answered as he picked up a cup and poured himself some coffee.

"I need you to go relieve Luther," Bell advised the man. "And have Harvey relieve Carl."

"You sure you don't want 'em in here for the night?" Castle asked as he took a sip. "We're gonna need everybody to be fresh for the drive tomorrow."

"Not this soon after a raid," Bell pointed out. "I don't want to be caught by surprise."

Castle snickered at the notion. "There ain't nobody coming for those cattle, Bell. We left that ranch a mess when we took 'em. You ain't got nothing to worry about. They're too scared to come here and try to get 'em back."

Bell looked out over the herd as he sighed. "Let's hope you're right."

Will checked his rifle and slid it back into the scabbard, and then pulled his revolver and checked it, too, before replacing it in its holster. He took one final glance over at Laughing Otter and when no words were spoken, he kicked the buckskin into action. He didn't like his odds of getting the horses out of Bell's possession but, at the same time, he could not ask any of them to risk being injured or killed because of a problem that he created. If he died, it would be by his own hands. And going against Bell and his men alone was almost a guarantee of failure.

He walked the buckskin down the hill and into the outer edge of Hangman's Gulch. He remembered where Bell's camp had been, but he wasn't sure exactly where he needed to go to get to it since his memory had been somewhat distorted from the beating he had endured at the hand of Bell's men.

As he entered the gulch, he turned to see where

Laughing Otter and his men were positioned. He was not shocked to see that none of the Lakota were anywhere within sight. *They didn't waste any time backing down.*

Will reluctantly started the buckskin through the winding dry creek bed, deeper into the gulch. Knowing what to expect, he would be on lookout more this time for men on the top of the rock faces. He would also pay more attention to his back trail in the hopes that no one would sneak up on him like they had before.

Will had no plan. When confronted, he doubted Bell or his men would give him any considerations since the last time they had met, Walks With Horse had killed one of them. He was going into this blind and alone.

He had wandered for a short time when he felt as if eyes were on him. Whether it was paranoia or a justified stance, it didn't matter. He would do what he could and see what happened. Determined not to repeat his mistakes from when he had come here before, he stopped the buckskin and waited, pulling his rifle in the process while watching above him, with a round already chambered to avoid making his presence known anymore than necessary. He watched.

He waited.

His instincts were telling him that he was not alone. He had learned long ago to listen to them because, more than once, doing so had saved his life.

As he turned a particularly shape corner in the dry creek bed, something told him to pause. He couldn't explain it, but he suddenly felt very vulnerable. His eyes darted from one side of the rock face to the other. His senses were heightened. He felt a lump forming in his throat where there had not been one. His breathing accelerated as a pronounced bead of sweat trickled slowly down his temple, building momentum as it fell. He suddenly felt the sweat soaking through his shirt and sticking to his back. His heart was racing. Is this where he would die?

High above Will, a man with a rifle was taking position. He had been scaling the tops of the rock wall since spotting Will's appearance in search of a better spot from which to ambush him. His orders from his boss, Bell, were perfectly clear. Anyone coming into the gulch before they could take the herd away was to be shot on sight. No questions asked.

The man took a spot at a point in the rocks that jetted out from the rock face and cradled himself into a nook as Will became more exposed. The man smiled at his luck. Once he was positioned, he raised his rifle to fire as a hand suddenly cupped over this mouth from behind at the same time that a knife blade was buried into the small of his back. The man gasped quietly as he felt the life draining out of him until his body went limp, while the hand was released from his mouth and began pulling the man's dead body back across the top of the rocks and out of sight. Will glanced up in the direction where he imagined he had seen the glimpse of a shadow of someone, but there was nothing to see. He slowly moved on.

He rounded the blind corner, expecting to come upon someone, but to his surprise, the trail was empty. He walked the buckskin, being cautious and quiet while he spanned the walls for Bell's men.

Just ahead of him, Jed Castle had a rifle barrel pointed out from the rocks, aiming right for Will, waiting for him to get a little closer and more exposed for an easier, more certain shot. He had just lined up his sights on Will when he heard the swoosh of an arrow as it embedded itself into the side of his neck, tearing out his windpipe and rendering him from uttering a sound. Castle clutched at his throat, trying to yell out, but the only sound he heard was the gurgling of his blood spilling from his neck wound and dripping onto the front of his shirt and the rocks below him. His rifle slid from his hands onto the rocks as he frantically clawed at the arrow protruding from both sides of his neck, his body going limp as he fell forward into the massive pool of blood that had already collected there. As his body exhaled for the last time, two Lakota slipped behind him, making their way silently across the top of the rock wall. Across the trail from them, four more Lakota were making their way down the opposite side.

Will continued easing his way deeper into the

gulch, his senses heightened by the lack of resistance he had expected, but for some reason, had not encountered. He could tell from where he was that he was not far from Bell's camp. Since he had not faced anyone on the rock walls, he replaced his rifle back into its scabbard and pulled his revolver, preferring it for close quarters as the buckskin carried him deeper into the gulch. Up ahead and just around the next bend in the trail, two of Bell's men waited as they heard the faint hooves of a horse on the parched rock floor of the dry creek bed.

"There's that drifter," one of the two men, Harvey, whispered excitedly to the man, Luther, that he had been sent to relieve.

Luther was confused as he watched Will continue his slow approach. "Why haven't we heard shooting before now?" He whispered in return while he leaned forward as he continued to stare Will down intently. "Are those boys sleeping again when they're supposed to be on lookout?"

He waited for a response from Harvey, but his friend did not answer. "What's the matter with you, Harvey? You ain't gonna say..." his words stopped as he glanced back at Harvey, who was sitting up, his eyes widened from terror, clutching his slit throat as blood oozed from between his fingers and quickly saturated his shirt. Laughing Otter was directly behind Harvey with a bloodied knife in his right hand staring at Luther with cold, dead eyes. Luther gasped at the man's appearance as the brave's left hand came swinging down with a tomahawk to the bridge of Luther's nose, creating the resounding cracking of bones being broken and sent piercing into his brain. Luther exhaled a dull grunt as he fell over dead onto his side on the rocks, his eyes still open wide in shock.

The braves continued easing their way across the rocks until they could see the trail opening up before them. They could hear the soft exchange between the cattle as they grazed long before they spotted them. Laughing Otter came up behind several of the braves and laid down next to them as he, too, watched over Bell's camp. They saw that there were seven or eight more men scattered throughout the camp and one disappeared into a small cave.

The braves took their positions all around on the outer rim of the small canyon, waiting for the sign to attack. They could not hear Will's horse approaching over the rustling of the cattle, but they knew he would appear at any second.

When he did, that would be their sign

CHAPTER TWENTY-TWO

Will had started to believe that he had been too late to stop Bell from carrying the horses to sell when he thought he heard the bellowing of cattle up ahead. The confusing sound stopped him in his tracks as he pulled the buckskin back sharply. He listened again and realized that what he heard was the unmistakable sound of cattle. *He had expected to hear horses moving about, but cattle? And why had he still not seen any lookouts?*

He chose to dismount and use the reins of the buckskin to lead him away from where he was going, towards the small canyon. He would feel better going the rest of the way on foot without fear of making the buckskin an easy target.

Will crouched and slipped undetected up to the entrance of the canyon where he could see the cattle mulling about with the horses mingled in with them. He took his position behind a rock and drew his revolver as he waited and pondered his next move.

From his vantage point, Will could see the entrance to the cave that he remembered Bell had frequented while they were holding him hostage. He glanced over at the men he could see, but none of them were Bell. Chances were, Bell was still inside the cave.

Will knew there was only one thing he could do. His only chance against so many men was to slip in and take Bell prisoner and use him to free the horses. If everything went well, he would be able to slip out of the canyon with the horses and Bell. Somewhere in there, he would need to scatter their horses to prevent them from following them to rescue their boss. If things went south, he would not make it to the first horse before they cut him down. As much as he hated the notion, he had no other choice.

He studied the layout briefly. The only way to the cave meant he would need to slip around to the left and skirt the herd and come up to the side of the cave next to the corral. But he did not like that option because it left too many open places where he could be spotted. His only other option: go through the herd.

He glance around the rim of the canyon, but he did not see any of Bell's men posted there. If he stayed down, it was possible he could maneuver his way through the cattle to the other side. The far side of the cattle was close to the cave entrance. If he took his time and didn't stir the cattle too much, there was a good chance he could slip into the cave without being seen. From there, he would have to rely on nothing more than dumb luck to make it out of there alive.

Relying on his patience, Will waited until some of the cattle eased their way over close to the rocks that were shielding him and saw his chance. He slipped into the herd and paused. No gunfire. He had not been seen.

The cattle were somewhat restless, as if they somehow knew that trouble was just on the horizon. He had to act fast before the herd became spooked. If that happened, being in the midst of them would be disastrous for him since he would easily become trampled before he could react and get out of there safely.

Will slowly made his way through the herd, taking his time and making sure not to push the cattle, easing his way through them as an opening appeared. He paused once, feeling as if he had been spotted by one of Bell's men, but the man did not react. After a few tense seconds, he assumed he was safe. Before long, he had crossed through the end and was in front of the cave entrance.

He waited for the right time to move and when he thought it was clear he took one final glance and made a run for it, darting into the cave entrance and stopping a few feet in, pressing his back against the darkened wall and listening. Nothing. No commotion. No detection.

After a final glance outside, he turned to continue in. He had only taken two steps when a man stepped out of the shadows directly in front of him. The man stopped abruptly, as surprised at seeing Will as he was at seeing him. As the man went off his gun, Will swung hard, connecting a left to the man's cheek and causing him to stagger. The punch was not solid, but it took the man off his feet long enough for Will to step forward and hit him on the head with the barrel of his gun. All Will heard was the resounding grunt from the man as he fell to the ground.

"Arturo?" a man called out from inside the cave. Will knew it was the voice of Bell.

Will slipped back into the shadows and waited. A moment later, Will watched as Bell appeared, gun in hand, slowly walking towards the opening. He did not see Will until he was on him and he felt the barrel of Will's gun in his side.

"Drop it," Will advised him sternly as he jabbed the barrel into Bell's side to prove he had the drop on him. Bell froze and slowly turned his head to face Will.

"Well, if it isn't the drifter," he spouted with a coy smile as Will reached over and took his gun from him, and slipped it into his waistband. "I take it you came to retrieve your horses. I'm not really surprised to see you here, but I am surprised at how you got past my lookouts."

"Guess they were asleep on the job," Will responded sarcastically.

Bell did not get pulled into the subject. "I don't see how you think you're going to get out of here alive, much less with those horses. My men will shoot you before you get even one of them out of here."

"You let me worry about that, Bell," Will said through a hardened face.

"Oh, I'm not *worried* about it," Bell proclaimed. "I'm wildly curious."

"Get moving," Will instructed him, pointing his gun in the direction of the entrance. Bell scoffed and then started walking ahead of Will. As soon as Bell was clear of the cave entrance, he suddenly dove off to the right.

"Man in the camp!" He yelled as he disappeared behind several horses that were tied off. The sudden move startled Will and left him frozen in place, not sure what to do. A bullet ricocheting off the rock beside him startled him back. He slid behind a small rock in front of the entrance and waited. He could see several of Bell's men scrambling to find cover.

The gunfire, along with the commotion, had started making the cattle restless. Their movements were becoming erratic as they began stirring more from the excitement. Will kept an eye out, waiting for the men to descend upon him. He caught a glimpse of a man running from behind some rocks to a wagon positioned off to his right. Before he could react, he saw another man skirting the outside of the

herd, trying to maneuver himself closer to get a
better shot. Will tried to aim while the man was out
in the open, but some of the cattle got in his way
before he could and he could not get a clear shot. A
bullet chipped away at the rock that was shielding
him. Another bounced off the dirt far enough away
from him not to matter. He suddenly wished he had
never heard of the wild horses.

He was trying to pinpoint where Bell's men were
when he heard two simultaneous thuds and then a
muffled groan coming from behind him. He whipped
his head around to see the man he had encountered
in the cave standing a few yards behind him with two
arrows buried deep in his chest. The man tried to
take another step, but his legs gave way and he fell
backwards into the dirt. Will was as shocked as the
expression on the man's face.

Lakota.

He had lost track of the man who had been
working his way around the herd until he saw him
running between rocks, making his way closer to
surround Will and get a better shot at him. Will
started to aim at the man when a bullet went through
his right arm just above the elbow, causing him to
drop his revolver. He responded by grabbing his arm
with his free hand as blood started running down his
forearm towards his hand. Will reached to retrieve
the revolver, but a bullet from Bell came dangerously
close to taking his hand off, so he was forced to
abandon it. He slid back behind the rock just as Bell

delivered another shot that also barely missed hitting its target.

Will reached into his waistband and pulled Bell's revolver with his left hand as he cut his eyes at the man coming around the herd. The man was advancing, but Will could not get a clear enough shot. He was trying to think of a way out from in front of the cave when he saw the man start to make a run for it across an open space. As the man stood, a brave came up from behind him and clubbed him in the back of the head with a tomahawk. Will watched as the brave delivered several more blows at the fallen man before he looked up and then disappeared back into the rocks.

The camp was engulfed in chaos as Bell's men fired at the Lakota with an occasional shot taken at Will. The cattle and horses had become so distraught at the gunfire and close fighting that they started to move towards the dry creek bed and down the trail away from the camp.

Will began to search the moving sea of animals for Bell, but there was too much going on and in the confusion, he didn't see Bell until he watched him riding off on a horse in the midst of the scattered herd.

Will frantically glanced around for another saddled horse and after spotting one, had taken a step towards it, when one of Bell's men, Jacobs, appeared and started wrestling the frantic horse to try to calm him down enough so he could climb into the saddle.

He held the horse by the reins as the animal tried to pull away from him, moving in a circular pattern to prevent Jacobs from putting his foot in the stirrup. Will had almost made it over to his horse when a brave appeared and tackled Jacobs, knocking him to the ground and landing on top of him. Will grabbed the reins and tried to settle the horse down as Jacobs screamed from the brave's knife penetrating his chest. It took several seconds for Will to finally get his foot in the stirrup, but he managed to swing into the saddle and take off after Bell.

A mixture of frightened cattle and horses filled the gulch, their deafening calls and a uniform chorus of bellows filling the air and drowning out everything around them. The narrow gulch was no match for the sheer volume of animals trying to move through such a bottleneck area, making his pursuit of Bell even more difficult.

Bell turned around and fired at Will, missing him, but not by much, his aim thrown off by stray cattle bumping into his horse. Will tried to steady his left hadn't enough to get off a shot, but his aim was interrupted by cattle running into his horse, too. He stuffed the revolver down into his waistband and decided to wait until they were clear of the cattle to return fire. He grabbed the reins with his left hand and urged his horse on, keeping a watchful eye on Bell as the gap between the two men continued to widen because of the frantic herd. With so many cattle between them, if he was not stopped soon, Bell would reach the edge of the gulch and have a substantial lead in getting away. Will could not let that happen.

Off in the distance, Will looked past Bell and saw a horse fast approaching them, but he could not make out the rider. He watched as Bell fired at the rider and then as the rider continued heading directly towards him. Bell got off several more shots before the rider pulled back their bow and launched an arrow that struck Bell's torso before he fell from his horse amid the stampede of cattle and his horse was lost in the group. Will continued riding towards the rider until he was close enough to see that it was Walks With Horse.

CHAPTER TWENTY-THREE

Will was relieved to see his friend as the two men closed the distance between them. They had to wait briefly for the remainder of the herd to pass them before they could turn their horses to one another. Walks With Horse rode up to greet Will, a faint smile on his face at seeing him.

"I didn't think I'd ever see you again," Will admitted as he pulled his horse to a stop next to Walks With Horse.

"Been watching you, Will Travis," the old man said. "Saw you at Lakota camp. Followed you back here."

"So it *was* you that I saw outside the tepee," Will stated with a confirming grin and a nod. "I knew that was you."

"Walks With Horse not go into camp. Must stay away from Lakota or make them sick."

"I understand."

Will started to say something when he saw Laughing Otter and the other braves walking out into the gulch where the cattle and horses had been, not having lost a single brave in the fight. He was still surprised at their appearance there to help him. He turned his horse towards the group with Walks With Horse following right behind him. When he met up with Laughing Otter, he dismounted and walked over to him.

"I didn't know you were coming to help me," Will admitted. "Thank you."

"I did not want to tell you, Will Travis, because I had to see if your heart was pure and if you were willing to return horses like you said. You coming in here alone shows you are honorable man and you speak the truth. Your life is spared, but only if you promise not to speak of Kawnteenowah again."

"Thank you," Will answered as he offered his hand. Laughing Otter hesitated just a second and then shook.

"We go now," Laughing Otter spoke. "Take horses back to canyon." He turned and motioned to the braves who nodded and split up to retrieve the horses they had been riding. Will turned to Walks With Horse just in time for the old man to collapse onto the ground. Will rushed over to him as Laughing Otter and the others saw what was happening and gathered around him. Will caught Walks With Horse's head before it hit the ground. It was then that he saw the blood on the front of Walks With Horse's shirt.

"Why didn't you tell me you were shot?"

"Does not matter," Walks With Horse said in a weakened breath. "I am old. It is my time to take a horse into the spirit world." He coughed deeply, almost to the point of choking, before he could catch his breath again. "Have been sick many days. Soon, sick no more."

"I'm sorry I got you into this," Will admitted, feeling helpless.

"Walks With Horse has friend in Will Travis." He patted Will on his chest as his head slowly turned away and his eyes closed.

Will stared down at the old man. "Yes, you do."

Will Travis followed Laughing Otter back and helped drive the horses back to the Lakota tribe, leaving the stolen cattle scattered on the prairie just outside of Hangman's Gulch. They also carried Walks With Horse back to the tribe for burial. After a day of preparation, Will was allowed to stay behind for Walks With Horse's burial ceremony.

Will watched as all the tribal preparations were made. Walks With Horse was wrapped in fine clothing and then wrapped tightly in robes and buried, with Two Elk performing the ceremony. Drums played and the members of the tribe chanted as his body was released from the tribe and his spirit sent into the spirit world. One of the horses Will had taken, a spirited white mare, was designated for Walks With Horse and was adorned with ceremonial dressings and paint, and after receiving Two Elk's blessing, was released onto the prairie. Will marveled at the complexity and grandness of the ceremony and thought it befitting of such a good man. He found himself grieving for his friend.

As Walks With Horse's steed was released, Will and the tribal members watched as it ran across the vast openness of the prairie and out of sight. Then the tribe dispersed and Will went back to Two Elk's teepee, at his invitation, and talked until he was eating dinner with the two men.

"Where will you go now, Will Travis?" Laughing Otter asked him as they sat around the fire with Two Elk, eating.

"I don't know," Will answered reluctantly. "I don't have a ranch to go back to," he admitted. "Even if I did, I don't have the money to save it."

"You have become friend of Lakota. You are welcome to stay here until you decide what you will do," Laughing Otter relayed the message from Two Elk. Just then, the teepee opened and the young woman who had treated Will's head wound, Gray Wolf, came in with more food. She sat down the dishes and then stole a quick glance at Will, a smile forming on her face as Will returned the gesture before she slipped back out of the teepee. The exchange was not lost on Two Elk or Laughing Otter.

Two Elk (Lakota) "....... ...."

"Two Elk thinks you have someone else who would like to see you stay awhile," Laughing Otter translated. Will glanced at Laughing Otter and smiled.

"What will you do with cattle that bad men took?" Laughing Otter asked.

"I don't know," Will spoke. "I can't drive them back by myself. I'm not even sure where they came from, and if I try to bring them in, the authorities might think I'm the one who stole them."

"You do not know where they came from?"

"No, but it has to be somewhere close by," Will answered. "I saw the brand. I should be able to ask around and find out who they belonged to."

Several days later, Will rode out to the nearest town of Johnson City and inquired about the stolen cattle. After tracking down the marshal, he was told about how rustlers had stolen cattle from the Triple Q Ranch and killed the owner and his ranch hands in the process. Will advised the marshal where the cattle were and if he could bring them in.

After making the proper arrangements, the marshal helped round up some men to go with Will and bring the cattle back to the ranch. With the owner deceased, Will talked with the bank and the land office and made arrangements to take over the Triple Q and use the sale of some of the cattle to settle his debt back in town.

A little more than two months passed as Will settled into his new ranch life. The ranch was just less than a day's ride from the Lakota camp, giving him a chance to go by and see Gray Wolf on a regular basis. On a particularly special trip to see Grey Wolf, Will had finally worked up the courage to ask Two Elk if he could marry her.

As he rode into the camp for the wedding, Grey Wolf was sitting next to a fire waiting for him. She smiled when they exchanged looks. As he rode up, he touched the necklace around his neck that Walks With Horse had given him. He wished his friend could have been there to see him marry and wondered how far the spirit horse had taken him.

———

Lee Everett has many more books for you to read! Visit his Amazon page at https://www.amazon.com/Lee-Everett/e/B07Z3BFKGL

Made in the USA
Middletown, DE
19 May 2022